SHOOT!

Also by Jay Cronley

Walking Papers
Funny Farm
Quick Change
Cheap Shot
Screwballs
Good Vibes
Fall Guy

SHOOT!

Jay Cronley

St. Martin's Press
New York

Design by Nancy Resnick

Library of Congress Cataloging-in-Publication Data

Cronley, Jay.
    Shoot / Jay Cronley.—1st ed.
        p.   cm.
    ISBN 0-312-15655-3
    I. Title.
PS3553.R544S48   1997
813'.54—dc21   96-6558
                                                                CIP

First Edition: June 1997

10   9   8   7   6   5   4   3   2   1

I would like to use this dedication page to speak positively about hip replacement surgery for dogs. I just got my springer spaniel a new steel hip at the veterinary hospital at the University of Missouri in Columbia. My springer had hip dysplasia and couldn't walk. Now he can fly. After the surgery, you write a book to pay for it.

JOE AND CAROLYN
The television room of their home on a decent fall Saturday afternoon

"Joe? Can I talk to you a minute?"

"Oh, Carolyn, *Jesus,* sweetheart, you're turning another of our moments together into a *New Yorker* cartoon. I, in my leather chair and matching ottoman, watching the last five seconds of an absolutely great college basketball game on the new picture-in-a-picture television set, with two naked women looking needy on the small screen in the corner. You, standing next to me, at this doubly critical instant, wanting to *figure out* something. Gosh, honey, son of a bitch. Please don't do this until somebody on the screen gets a little lucky."

"This isn't a *New Yorker* cartoon. In a *New Yorker* cartoon the one in the leather chair would be wanting to watch the last five seconds of a church service."

"Church service? What, Carolyn, I don't get it."

"That's the point of a *New Yorker* cartoon, Joe, to make the reader feel in need of enlightenment. Every once in a while they throw in an easy cartoon that everybody can get, you know, something political or a joke about a twelve-step support group. Let the readers think they're improving. Then *pow,* here comes another of those cartoons that can't be gotten, one of a familiar scene but with dialogue that doesn't seem to match. You know. Two people sitting at a breakfast table. The woman says, 'Guess what, I'm not meditating today.' And so you have to keep reading the magazine in hopes of one day getting them all. Which you never can. I think what they do on two of their cartoons is flip-flop the cutlines. But it's pretty shrewd marketing, don't you think?"

"What is it you want, Carolyn? And for how many minutes do you want it?"

"You don't like me much anymore, do you Joe."

"Jesus God. All I can say is I'll like you more in five seconds, Carolyn. Five-point-seven seconds, actually."

"All right, Joe. I'll wait. . . . ."

. . . .

. . . .

". . . There was a horn. So what happened with your game?"

"It's not *my* game. It's the whole damn country's. It's important to dozens of millions."

"Fine."

"We're in OT."

"OT."

"Yeah."

"Let me guess."

"Sure, go ahead."

"OT, OT, OT, let's see, OT . . . . . Optimum, no, OT, Occasional, no, T, Transition, Translation . . . . . Optical Translation . . . . ."

"Very close, Carolyn, damn good try."

". . . . . Overt, no, no, Christ, OT, OT, *Open Tournament.*"

"Sharing a pastime can be very rewarding, can't it."

"What, then."

"Overtime. The last shot was missed. The game ended tied. They play five more minutes."

"Lucky you. Lucky America."

"What exactly is it that you want, Carolyn?"

"You want a divorce, Joe?"

"Oh, God in heaven, Carolyn. What have I ever done to deserve this?"

"You married me."

"..... That's the best answer there's ever been to a question, Carolyn. It has everything, truth, irony, sarcasm, a dark wit......"

"Well, *do* you want a damn divorce?..... It would be expensive, wouldn't it..... having half *alone* sounds like a lot less than having half together....."

"Half of what?"

"Half of everything..... And stop looking at me like that..... Goddamn it, Joe, *quit* it....."

"..... I'm just being attentive..... respectful of the speaker."

"No. Bullshit. You're trying to frighten me. I've seen that look a lot lately, Joe. I've had dreams about it. A nightmare. It's been coming back more nights than not. You staring unblinkingly. Fiercely. It's a very severe sensation. Very real."

"Carolyn, it's simply a look of spiritual confusion, of wondering how a good God could condone anything like this kind of timing....."

"Maybe *I* want a divorce, Joe."

"..... Yeah?"

"Quit *looking* at me like that....."

"Carolyn, please suggest to me a look to put on my face to acknowledge the receipt of torture....."

"Look *down*..... and push the goddamn mute button on the television, all right?"

"Sure, no problem, Carolyn, there you go."

"Thank you."

"You're welcome."

"Now I suppose you'll pout."

"No. I'll turn the sound back on the second this conversation becomes unproductive, the instant it looks like you're jealous of my hobby....."

"Well, that doesn't seem fair, I mean, what's one second....."

"The tenth second, then, how's that?"

"Oh. Better. I guess."

"Why is it that you think you want a divorce, Carolyn?"

"Because of my heart, Joe, the way it feels like dead weight sometimes. . . . . Now, goddamn it, you *blink,* I mean it, Joe, you can't look at me like that. . . . ."

"That's six horseshit seconds."

"It's not cumulative; it's ten consecutive bad seconds. . . . ."

"No, and that's nine. . . . ."

"Joe, don't, we *have* to talk. . . . ."

"Bingo. . . . ."

". . . . . *and Corey's shot bounced high off the back of the rim, that's four in a row they've missed from behind the three-point line* . . . . ."

While Joe watched the last of the basketball game on which he had bet two thousand dollars, nineteen hundred and forty-five of which he didn't seem to quite have, Carolyn went out and put into her system a little of the cocaine on which she had recently spent twenty-five hundred dollars. It was that or do something like write a novel, and she didn't have any ideas or a particular way with words because all she did was sell computers and their programs for a living.

So . . . . .

It was have some cocaine or go back to college at the age of whatever she was—thirty-five, thirty-six, somewhere in there; thirty-seven if somebody wanted to get technical—and get a master's in something she no longer had an interest in, like speech therapy. Oh boy, *there* was a major they should outlaw, speech therapy, the female equivalent of PE, of studying physical education, what bony-headed football players did.

It was that or shout it out in divorce court, dig and scratch for dollars, fight for every penny, erase all memories of their good times back before they each went stale; a terrible thing, that, wasn't it, defaming the good times that didn't have a thing in the world to do with these.

It was that or run away from home at the age of goddamn *whatever,* and live off the land out in a goofy place like the

Southwest where all the wrinkled-up ex-hippies with barely enough brain cells left sat on rocks trying to remember the good times and making up crap instead.

It was that or watch some television.

It was that or go buy another cat.

It was that or get drunk, a pain. *Being* drunk was all right, it was fine, but getting there was a rough trip in coach. It took too long.

It was that or do some work, get on the horn and try to sell some computer machines, try to put some big wheels on the info autobahn.

Next.

It was that or plant some more flowers out back. Every time Carolyn got depressed she would go to her garden and attempt to lose herself in the unsoiled beauty of God's little miracles, the flowers. The process of seeking relief in the garden started about a year ago. There was something spiritual about rooting around in the dirt, with the forever-old thrill of starting life with your fingers, though it be but a crocus, still holding water. But what began as a charming English country garden had now come to resemble more the dense courtyard of a country insane asylum that had been planted by patients, with vines and stalks and bushes and shrubs growing rough, and with bees and wasps and centipedes and all manner of things with stingers and poisons lurking just off the cobblestone pathway.

It was that or kill him.

It was that or go to the health club and exercise; oh, *please*, was she *that* desperate for relief? Sweating with unknown members of the opposite sex, lame, wishful-thinking members: Contemporary life came no hokier. At least this socially accepted form of spreading and shaking it for strangers kept numerous aging broads brimming with undeserved self-esteem.

It was basically a little drug action or nothing for Carolyn this afternoon.

Not that she couldn't quit the instant God got around to

helping her with a couple dozen problems, the second she felt some hope.

Joe lost the two thousand dollars he had bet on the basketball game, plus a commission of two hundred dollars to the book-maker, for a total sucker punch of twenty-two hundred. He lost when a player from the team he had bet on shot the basketball toward the goal with two seconds left in overtime. It goes in and he wins. Simple. The basketball Joe had bet on hit first the front of the rim and then the back of the rim. Then it hit one side of the rim and then the other side. A shot hitting all four sides of the hoop, the dramatic nature of the basketball bouncing around up there as the final horn went off, it caused the announcer to say "Crap, man," on network television. Then the shot fell away from the goal and the announcer apologized first for saying "crap," and then he apologized for saying that circles, or rims, had _sides._ An engineer had told him through the headphones that only straight lines had sides. But hey, the announcer said, circles did so have sides, _insides_ and _outsides._

Boy did they ever, Joe thought.

The loss brought Joe's bottom gambling line to ground zero, to maximum intensity, to eighteen thousand the other way, eighteen to his bookmaker.

Plus his wife was talking divorce.

Good Christ.

I am one sick, miserable, compulsive, obsessive gambling lunatic, he thought, staring at the small screen on the picture-in-a-picture television set where not two, and not three, but _four_ whole lesbians were rubbing up and kissing up one another, which was a good thing because otherwise Joe's large and frightening and unmanageable gambling debt, on top of his poor situation at home, might have brought to the front some life-threatening thoughts.

CAROLYN AND VINCENT FRANCIA
Locked up during the noon hour

"God, what an awful place this is."

"Well Jesus, I'm humiliated. Should I call the gardener and have him sprint up something fragrant?"

"I'm sorry. . . . . I didn't mean . . . . ."

"Or maybe I should call a guard and have him stomp a few fucking cockroaches."

"No. . . . ."

"What is it that bothers you the most about our humble shelter here?"

"You mean it? You want a serious answer?"

"Yes, sure."

"Well. There's no color."

"You know why that is?"

". . . . . No."

"Take a guess."

"Oh. It would be too cheerful?"

"That, yeah. You'd piss off all the victims. And the morons would eat the paint. Old paint."

"I'm really sorry. I don't mean to be snotty. . . . ."

"Let me tell you something, my attractive woman friend with nice legs, from what I can see. If you think *this* is bad, then you better lead a good and lucky life, sweetheart, because for a goddamn stinking miserable prison, this place is not too bad of a deal, actually."

". . . . . Really?"

"Oh yes, sure. The bugs here, see that one by your foot. That's the way, just scoot it aside, don't smash it, we can use all the company we can get. See there, it's got the right number of legs. A nice crisp and shiny shell. There are no mutant or malnourished bugs in this facility, my dear."

". . . . . Okay. . . . ."

"Now there's a state prison in Illinois where the toilets don't have water in them all the time. You can imagine what fun that is. Some idiot drowned himself in his pot, honest to God, the stinking toilet water. Wedged his head down in there, got it stuck somehow. So they only ran the water through the pipes twice a day."

"I'd still hate to see a place worse than this."

"Well, as honest-looking a person as you are, I wouldn't worry. Now what can I do for you? You're not one of those journalists or anything like that, are you?"

"No."

"I get them, looking to do old-time shoot-'em-up stories, you know, the-end-of-an-era pieces, like I'm some kind of relic. Some kind of criminal. I don't like journalists. I have found it in my experience to note that most of those pricks are more interested in furthering their cheeseball little careers than they are in informing the masses of the God's truth."

"I'm not a journalist."

"Good. Now. Are you a relative?"

"I'm sorry . . . . . what?"

"Like a cousin of mine. I don't want to be having any sexual thoughts about relatives. It's not my mentality."

"No. We're not related."

"Good. Now tell me what you want, why you're here."

"All right. I want somebody killed."

. . . .

. . . .

"What's *that* fucking supposed to mean?"

"Just exactly what it sounds like. It's hard enough saying it once. It would make me extremely nervous saying it over and over. So please believe me."

"Believe you? . . . . ."

"Yes."

". . . . All right."

"*God.* Thanks."

"Now I want you to listen close to what I have to say."

"I am."

"I have no sense of humor. None. The last thing I can even remember laughing at was a business competitor's great misfortune. He backed a car over his mother, who had bent down to pick up a quarter. Ran right over her head in one of those Lincoln Town Cars. It's black humor that I can relate to. Absolutely none of that horseshit practical-joke kind of mentality."

"This is no joke."

"It better not be."

"It isn't."

"It better not be a joke *or* the truth."

". . . . Well . . . . ."

"It had better be a *mistake.*"

"It's . . . . . not."

"You sure?"

"Yes."

"Well then, give me a second here."

"Okay. Sure. Listen, I'm . . . . ."

"Be quiet.

. . . .

. . . .

. . . .

. . . .

"All right then. What's your name?"

"Carolyn."

"Last name."

"Rogers. No. It isn't. That was a lie. I just made it up. I don't want to give my real last name to you."

"What are you doing here? With me? And lean over the table so you don't have to talk so loud."

"I want somebody killed. And what better place to find somebody in that business than . . . . . here. I mean, what am I supposed to do, barhop?"

"You know something?"

"I'm not sure. . . . ."

"It's times like this when I wish I *had* a sense of humor. Because this might be pretty damn funny."

"Well, whatever else it is, it's also the truth."

"All right then. Fine. Only, I'm not in here on any kind of *killing* thing. I'm in here on a tax thing. An oversight."

"I know."

"You do?"

"Yeah."

"How's that, Carolyn?"

"I read about you at the newspaper morgue. The microfilm room. It's where I found you. Just randomly going through back issues. You've been charged with two murders. Questioned in a few others. Never convicted. That's good. I mean, it's what I need. I don't want to talk to a *bad* killer."

. . . .

"You see that? I just laughed at something besides a natural disaster befalling a competitor."

"You looked a lot younger doing it. Today is the third. If you want to write it down for reference. See how long until the next one."

"You know what? I don't mind you."

"Excellent. Can you help me?"

"Oh, man. That. I don't know."

"What would it cost?"

"Well, I'd say around thirty-five thousand dollars."

"*Jesus.*"

"It's a pretty exclusive skill."

"Who do I call, then?"

"Tell you what. Let me think about it."

". . . . . Okay."

"Give me a number where you can be reached in the morning."

"All right. And thank you."

"Listen. Tell me what you think about this. Maybe we can have dinner sometime. I'm only sixty-two. And change."

". . . . . Well, sure."

"Great, that's just great. I'm out of here in a couple of months."

"So . . . . ."

"Wait. Sit back down a second. There's one thing I need to tell you before you go. If you're fucking with me in any way, shape, form, or manner, I'll poke your eyeballs out with my dick."

"I think I'd like to cancel our dinner engagement."

"There, you did it again, I'm smiling."

He had to be having sex with somebody.

Didn't he?

They only did it often enough to stay pissed off about how infrequently they were doing it, say, once a month.

So, since he had to be doing it, to get the revenge over and done with and out of the way, she took up with an attorney named Mark, a man seven years her junior; seven years and some noticeable IQ points.

God Almighty, they weren't making younger men like they used to, were they? She remembered younger men as being somewhat tougher. But then again, too, she had been younger herself when she had last messed with more youthful men.

They were making the current bunch of younger men handsome but fragile, family-business types scared of people working and playing more than a few miles from the hospital where they had been born.

Some recent journalism school graduate so proud of her

thighs, that was probably about Joe's speed down at the newspaper where he wrote editorials.

Revenge was *so* tiresome. It could just drain a person. So getting it over with before she officially needed it was sound psychologically. Instead of wasting time worrying about who he was doing, she was on Mark. A little guilt beat a little fear, it was that simple; you went with the most pleasurable pain. What was Joe supposed to say to the recent journalism school student with tight skin anyway—"No, I'm not brilliant, young woman, now would you put that halter top back on"? He'd better not have told her to put her shirt back on, not after she had come up with Markie baby.

After going to prison, she went to Mark's condo and tried to lose herself in his arms but succeeded only in losing a good earring.

Mark's mom had decorated his condominium in muted earth tones, and the whole place was so predictable, it was like screwing in a junior suite in a decent Dallas or San Antonio hotel; the condo was slick but had no personality.

There was just so much disappointment a person could take.

Ten minutes in, she broke off her absentminded sex and told Mark she was done with this, so long, and she left him standing and feeling confused and inadequate beneath a monstrous painting of a purple cactus.

He said wait, he wasn't sure he could live without her.

She said this was no concern of hers.

What a monumental and colossal drag it was to learn that your husband did you better than your more muscled and youthful insignificant ex-other.

"Joe?"

"Yeah."

"What's that static on the line?"

"My lungs."

"You're smoking again?"

"Cigar."

"I wanted to go over my schedule for the week. Let you know what's up."

"That's nice, Carolyn. What are you feeling guilty about?"

"Joe, do me a big favor, don't be an asshole for two minutes."

"Deal."

"I think I'll work late."

"Yeah? Tonight?"

"Yeah."

"There at your office?"

"Sure."

"Anybody else going to be there?"

"What in the hell kind of question is that. No, nobody is going to be here. Feel free to lower yourself down from the roof and peek in my window anytime you wish."

"How late you thinking about working?"

"Oh. Ten. Ten-thirty."

"You want me to bring some food by? Pizza, something like that?"

"No. I brought a sandwich."

"All right."

"What about you, Joe?"

"There's a game on."

"You're *kidding.*"

". . . . . No."

"You going to watch it alone?"

"I thought I'd have the Mormon Tabernacle Choir over and have some chips and dip. Course I'm going to watch it alone, Carolyn."

"Fair enough. Talk to you later."

"Have fun working, Carolyn."

"And good dribbling to you."

Her name was Lara and she was a recent journalism school graduate who thought he was one of the greatest living writers in America today. And if he didn't believe her, all he had to do was look at how impressed her naked breasts were. An editorial he had written the previous day about families living below the poverty level was so moving, she gave twenty-five dollars to a soup line. She was the fondest of the way he used humor to make serious points. His way with words was to make an unexpected one show up in a place you would least imagine. It wasn't like he had to search for the right words. It was like he charmed them into volunteering for duty. *Write* like him? Oh please. She would consider her career successful if she got to where she could *punctuate* like him. So should she put her top back on? No, she should take her pants off.

There in his office, after almost everybody else had gone, she was all that could make him forget that his life was in ruin.

She was twenty-two.

A year older, and even *she* might not have worked, might not have been enough.

DANNY AND CAROLYN
Near sundown in his new vehicle

"You know what I've been working on?"

"*No.* Jesus. No. Watch the road, Danny, okay?"

"I've been working on a suicide-looking thing."

"A what?"

"A way to make somebody being killed look like a suicide."

"I don't need anything like that. Come *on.* You're changing lanes without signaling."

"Well do you fucking mind if I *tell* you about what I've been working on?"

". . . . . No."

"Thank you very much."

"You're welcome."

"Don't do that. Don't say 'You're welcome' if somebody is using sarcasm. Sarcasm is like, unanswerable."

". . . . . All right."

"Thank you very much.

 . . . .

"Good. Now about the suicide. The suicide *note,* you understand, would be the kicker. The key. The note would be what made it suicide, the evidence that clinched it. The evidence that kept the police out, a note that was obviously written by the dead guy, a note that you could check and see was the same handwriting. Now. Listen to this. You know how to make the handwriting the same on the suicide note as it was in real life?"

"Sure."

".....*Sure?* What the hell is *sure* supposed to mean?"

"You force the person you're going to kill to write the note before you shoot him."

"Oh for the love of Christ."

"You know, signaling when you turn might help, Danny. The truck you turned in front of, missed you by two feet, tops....."

"You can't *force* somebody you're going to kill to write a suicide note."

"Why's that, Danny?"

"Because if he wrote the suicide note then you'd kill him for sure."

"I thought that was the whole point."

"*His* whole point would be staying alive. The *second* he wrote the suicide note, he's dead. No note, no dead."

"Whatever, Danny. I'm new at this."

"You use the *killer's* handwriting! Is that great or what. It came to me like *that* the other day."

"Over cocktails?"

"Over what?"

"Nothing."

"So here's the way it works. I go into a place, a house, an apartment, you know, a dwelling, and I take all the written examples of the one going dead. And I leave in their places my own damn handwriting. Letters. Notes. Grocery lists. Whatever you find around a house. Sure. Now, it's going to take some time and some effort. But it's worth it. It stops the police cold. Then after I put some of my handwriting around the house, I leave the suicide note also in my handwriting. 'Dear world: Fuck this, et cetera, et cetera, signed, Whichever.' By me. The police match the handwriting on the note with what's around the house, have an expert compare the writing, it's over. What do you think about that?"

"You're really making me nervous, looking at me while you're driving seventy-four."

"I always look at who I'm talking to. It's what a man does."

"I believe you're a man. I know it. So case closed, all right? Just watch the road. Please. And your wig is crooked. And those dark glasses at night might attract some unwanted attention."

"You keep this up, *dear,* and we just might have to get divorced. *Your* wig, it looks like you ought to be singing backup for some transvestites. What about my suicide note thing?"

". . . . . Well . . . . ."

"Now what's *that* supposed to mean?"

"I was just thinking out loud."

"What's to think about?"

"Checks."

"Checks? What checks?"

"Canceled checks. From the bank. What about the handwriting on them?"

"Well . . . . . fuck . . . . ."

"That's what I meant by *well.* . . . ."

"I have some canceled checks made, faked. Okay? Sure. There's fucking people having *dollars* made. A fucking lousy stupid check with a fake cancellation stamp on the back, how fucking hard could that be. . . . ."

"Could you please watch your language just a little bit, I can't focus on anything with you talking like that. . . . ."

". . . . . Boy oh boy, I can't wait to get to the prom so I can talk to some of the *guys.* So what about making some canceled checks?"

"It sounds like a good *Columbo.*"

". . . . . A *what?*"

"A *very* good one."

"But that buffoon Cyclops Columbo always *catches* them on that damn show. . . . ."

"Make a left here, Danny. . . . ."

"What was *that?*"

".....What? ....."

"That noise."

"What noise? Please. Stop creating this tension. I can't take much more....."

".....The dashboard. Under the dash. I heard a bad squeak."

".....Jesus, stop, Danny, what are you *doing?* ....."

"Pulling the car over."

"No. *Please.* There's a truck in the right lane....."

"Screw him. He hits me, I'll kill him, I mean it....."

"Get over now, Danny, it's clear all the way to the shoulder....."

".....You know what this thing cost?"

"Plenty, Danny. Come on, pull farther off the road, all right? This is how people get killed, parking too close to a damn freeway."

"Sixty-six, six, that's what it cost. For that, no squeaks now. Tomorrow. Ever. All right. I'm getting under the dash. You push right there in the middle when I say.....Hang on.....wait a second.....go ahead....."

".....I am....."

".....Push *harder.* ...."

".....I'm using both hands....."

".....Hit it....."

".....This doesn't look like average driving conditions to me....."

".....All right, all right, it's quit, you can stop pushing....."

"I thought you heard something outside the damn car, anyway, Danny."

"You know, now that you mention it, the noise did sound remotely catlike. I'm just a perfectionist, that's all. You should be glad of that as my employer. What's the traffic look like back there now?"

"After the cab."

"Got it.....She left me last week. Dee Dee. Just up and

walked out. It's why I bought this thing, to take my mind off her leaving."

"Right lane, Danny, right at the next exit. About three-quarters of a mile."

"Tell me one thing."

"I'll try."

"Why do women leave?"

"Oh. It's probably hormonal for the most part."

"That's exactly what I thought. In love. Out. Makes no sense."

"Only to women. And their gynecologists."

"Look at me. Look me in the eye."

"Sure thing. Take the next left."

"Do you think I got fucked paying sixty-six, six, for the premiere off-road vehicle that is equally at home pulling up in front of *Coppelia* as it is cooling its heels in the Snake River?"

". . . . . No."

"What's *Coppelia* anyhow?"

"A ballet."

"You don't think that behind the wheel of this I look like a yuppie half-fag type of person?"

". . . . . No, Danny, never."

"Then what does it make me look like?"

"I don't know. . . . . God . . . . . the Marlboro man."

"Jesus *Christ*. He died of lung cancer."

"Behind the wheel of your Range Rover you look like him long before he passed on."

"What'd you say to do at this corner?"

"Nothing. Just stop. That's it over there. South side. Third house in. Mossy-colored."

"I think I'll pull on down to the other end of the street where it's darker."

"Fine."

"Middle of the block."

"Okay, okay."

"He's inside there now?"

"Yeah. All night."

"What is he to you?"

". . . . . Nothing."

"No. I mean related-wise."

"I'm going to be his widow."

They sat on the dark end of the street a little bit and discussed a few important things, beginning with money.

Money was important to everybody, even to rich people pretending it wasn't.

It was at least quadruply important to people without that much.

Danny used to think that there were two things more important than money: love and happiness. But that turned out to be BS. Love and happiness were way too hard to find and keep. What was the divorce rate, anyway, half, 50 percent? But that figure used only one divorce per customer. Half the people had been divorced. But if you factored in all those who had been divorced two or three or more times, the rate would be around 80 percent.

Danny's divorce rate was 300 percent; he was a three-time user.

He had decided that money was easier to find than love and so was devoting all his creative energies in that direction.

Make some money.

Call some tramps.

Next question.

Money was so important in this day and age that discussing who had what coming made people edgy right off.

Danny and Carolyn got into it about money before he could get a CD going on the world-class sound system.

Danny asked for half of the thirty thousand dollars he had coming, but Carolyn said that she had thought it over and had decided to give him a fourth down, seventy-five hundred, the rest when the job was finished. They had agreed on half before. Carolyn had changed her mind, had violated their agreement, and it made Danny mad. He hit the dash. Fortunately it didn't squeak. He said if she wasn't careful, he'd rob her of the seventy-five hundred right now, and then where would she be?

Carolyn said that she had changed her mind precisely because of what he had just threatened, to rob her. Had she brought half, he probably would have taken it and put one through an ear. She hadn't known he'd turn out to be a fine, upstanding Range Rover–type gentleman.

So Danny took the seventy-five hundred-dollar bills.

Next, she gave him the key to the back door of the house. Her house. Their house. Danny was going to go in the back, unlocking it nice and easy, and then he was going to shoot Joe through the brain as he sat watching a stupid basketball game. Before leaving, Danny would break the back-door glass from the outside, making it appear to have been busted prior to a robbery that went violent.

Danny said he liked basketball and wondered who was on the tube tonight.

Carolyn ignored that and told him what to steal and said wait a minute, its value should come out of the balance that was due. Joe wore a watch that was worth fifteen hundred easily.

Danny thought that over and said yeah, Carolyn probably had a point about monies pouring in from secondary sources relating to this endeavor.

So exactly what percent of the life insurance would she be giving him?

This ended any discussion of monies paid and due.

JOE AND TISH
Her rented car, just after sundown

"It's pretty simple."
  "What is, Joe?"
  "This."
  "Yeah, I know."
  "It's her or me."
  "Who?"
  "Cut and dried."
  "What are you talking about?"
  "This."
  "What, Joe?"
  "I'm trying to explain what's going on."
  "I know what's going on. I'm killing your wife for forty thousand dollars, cash on the pecker-head."
  "But do you know *why?*"
  "No."
  "I'd like to tell you."
  "Okay, I guess."
  "It's her or me."
  "I don't care, Joe."
  "*I* care."
  "All right, all right."
  "If she doesn't die, *I* die. How do you like that?"

"Watch your beer, Joe, it's spilling on your jeans there."

"Okay, Tish. *Tish.* Is that really your name?"

"Yes."

"Well after tonight, it stops here, I'll tell you that for sure. I would never have anybody killed again. No matter how desperate or unhappy I became. I just want you to know I'm not a bad person."

"What in the hell do you think this is, a date?"

"You know how much I owe Cooper?"

"Yeah, Joe, eighteen thousand."

"I lost twelve straight basketball bets. Can you believe it?"

"Cooper said you stink."

"Oh he did, did he?"

"Yeah. He said you were one of the worst sports gamblers he's ever booked. He said his dog could pee on a team, you know, urinate on a parlay card, and Cooper said he could bet what came out the wettest and beat you."

"What else did he say? Did he talk about his being so lacking in height?"

"No, that was about it."

"He say anything about . . . . . what I owe?"

"Oh, that. Yeah. Sure. He mentioned that. How could he not? I mean, it's so *much.*"

"What did he say?"

"Something about how he hoped you'd pay on time."

"*Tish.* God all mighty. I like your legs. But it sounds like you should be tossing one out of the rough somewhere."

"I do play a lot of golf, Joe. Why don't you hand me that beer. I think you've had plenty. And you might stick your head out the window like a dog and get a couple of gulps of fresh air. You're all over the place."

"Well, I'm a little nervous. So why don't you just lift your skirt up a little, there's no doubt that would work miracles with my nerves."

"I'm going to warn you about that kind of talk right now, Joe. I've got a busy night's work ahead. I can't be distracted by nonsense. You can talk about my legs all you want. But the skirt-lifting dialogue is out. Otherwise I'll smack you right in the fucking mouth. This street runs into a one-way. What about it?"

"Take it."

"Now what about the money, the down payment you owe me?"

"It's right here. Eight thousand, five."

"But it was supposed to be ten, damn it."

"Hey, come on, a person has to eat."

"Eat what, Joe?"

"My words mostly. Another sports creditor was about to get pissed off and take some of my valuables. Like from my body . . . my eyes."

"You bet with somebody besides Cooper?"

"Last night. That's all. I had to. It was that or read a book."

"You understand that the rest is due the *second* the insurance money on her arrives."

"It goes without saying. Take the first alley to the right. . . . . No, that's a private drive, go on a little. . . . . Yeah, there. Listen, I'd like to ask you a question. Why do you do what you do?"

"Why do I kill people?"

". . . . . Yeah."

"Then say it. You're not watching this on television. You're participating in it."

"It's still pretty surreal, I'll tell you that. . . . ."

"*Say* it, Joe, right now, because you're a part of it."

". . . . . Why do you . . . . . kill people?"

"That's a good question. First, I have one for you. How in the world can a person make so many losing bets?"

"Oh. It's really pretty simple. First you move in with Carolyn."

"Now about your question. Why do I kill people. The answer is because I love money. I love houses where the surf breaks, and I love clothes made so well they seem to float an inch off your body. I can't do without orchestra seats and Lexuses. I've tried. And it hurts. I feel actual physical pain going cheap. I get headaches serving myself. Only the inbred don't enjoy travel. Now, being without talent or wealthy parents, I have found that there are three ways to make the money I need, Joe. One is by marrying rich men. The second is by divorcing them. The third is by killing people. And my God, divorce has become *so* hard. It's the drugs and alcohol screwing up the practice of divorcing worthless rich fuckers, Joe. There was a time, they'd just say so long and go out and make some more money. It's the second- and third-generation inherited rich making a shambles of marrying the wealthy. They're so goddamn tight. Second- and third-generation inheritors know that they have no skill and no right to the money, and the guilt they feel is oppressive. They know that once the money is gone, it's over, they haven't the ability to get it back. So when you sue one of those rich kids working for Pop, they don't say well, you got me, see you later. No. They weep. I even had one of them commit suicide on me the day after I sued him for divorce. They *stalk*, can you imagine such a thing. Faced with the loss of undeserved money, but nevertheless money that is the only defining point in their lucky and inconsequential existence, well, hell, they're liable to come at you with a razor blade in one hand and a cup of lye in the other. From my perspective, Joe, which is one of wishing to have as much money for as little effort as is possible, killing beats marrying, hands down and whistling. Any questions?"

"No. Jesus. You've frightened me. I can't concentrate on anything but the excellent shape of your calves."

"Thank you. Corner office there?"

"With the light on. Back entrance is open. Security is in a car, a guard drives around the whole complex. No discernible schedule."

"Fine. I'll put on a cute little short skirt and say I'm delivering a pizza and walk right in."

"Don't forget to rob the place."

"Burgle. And thanks for reminding me. Maybe I'd better write it down. Eat a mint. You smell like a bar."

Joe had the one calling herself Tish take him to a park and let him out so he could walk around some, telling her that he was getting sick to his stomach and might throw up.

What he was going to do was think hard about having his wife killed and then either return to the rented car or run the other way and forget it.

Having her killed so that he could start another life fresh and debt-free and with some money in his pocket sounded like a pretty good idea until it came time to go do it.

Tish in her wig and big glasses and floppy hat, she'd probably shoot and miss and be caught and Joe would go to prison for an attempted fresh start.

Tish had come into Joe's life when he told the one he owed money to, Cooper, that he didn't have the cash, that he couldn't pay. Cooper, who was short and soft and reminded Joe of a poisonous mushroom, said, well, maybe you should give it some more thought.

So he did.

He thought and thought and could only think of the one way out and asked Cooper if he knew anybody in the insurance business.

Selling insurance? Cooper wondered.

No, *causing insurance,* Joe told him.

Joe, like everybody else, had heard that under the right set of circumstances, or probably more accurately, under the *wrong* set of circumstances, people were capable of anything, even killing. But he hadn't much believed it. That was because life was decent. And now that it wasn't, now that life sucked like a big toilet plunger, he didn't know what to think.

So he walked around the park, trying to think of another way to get the money he didn't have, the woman he didn't have, the life. He took deep breaths of the nice fall air and was alert for the word of God, an intervention, a vision, telling him what to do now. He looked up every few yards, looked at the top of the tree-line, figuring that was where a message from God Almighty would come from, from slightly above.

What he found, between two large boulders, was a group of homeless substance abusers, five of them in number, four young, one on up there, probably around fifty years of age, though he was so weather- and vice-worn it was hard to tell. The younger people hanging out between the big rocks in the park appeared to be in their twenties and thirties and were tough-looking guys all.

Two young men smoked some marijuana, two drank beer, and the older person smoked a joint *and* drank beer, showing them what they could look forward to later in life if they played their trumps right.

Joe had brought with him from the rented four-door a beer of his own.

He told the others that he was feeling a little unsteady on his feet and asked if he could sit down a minute.

The older fellow said sure and asked if he could freshen Joe's beer. Joe nodded, not having any idea how that could be accomplished. The older man took Joe's can of beer and poured some cheap bourbon into it.

Joe said thanks and had a sip.

Bad.

Very bad.

But not wanting to seem ungrateful, Joe closed the back of his throat and refused to puke up what he had just swallowed.

The older man noticed Joe's obvious discomfort and said there was no need to put on airs, he was among friends, he could go ahead and throw up on himself if it felt like the thing to do.

Joe smiled without meaning it and said he was all right.

The older man poured some cheap whiskey into his own cheap beer and had a long swallow and said it tasted like donkey piss.

One of the others asked about the particulars of *that* chance encounter, about drinking donkey piss. Now horse piss, yes sure, knowing what that tasted like could happen to anybody. You're riding along at a dude ranch, riding through the aspen turning bright yellow, and a moose and her baby are in your path and your horse throws you and then gets nervous and pisses on you.

But come on now, who rides *donkeys.*

The older one comparing what he was drinking with donkey piss rolled his red eyes and said excuse me for working with the English language with these dopes. He had never drunk any donkey piss. He was simply making the point that donkeys were odd combinations, as were cheap beer and cheap whiskey.

All *right?*

Hey, yeah, one of the younger ones with a joint said, not bad, good thinking.

The older one said he had been married to the love of his life who got cancer and died in a two-month period, got a lump right at the base of her neck that grew and grew and fucking spread and killed her. Among others. Killed him some, too, it looked. This was what, fifteen years ago? Sure. Fifteen next month, actually. Now, he hadn't been a famous scientist or anything like, the horse crap you hear from many of the other sots on the walk. He had been an average salesman in an office supply store. And he didn't know much. But the one thing that he did know was that in this life you got one dog who could look right into your heart and convey such a pure and unconditional love and trust that you knew it could never be duplicated, not even close, and you got one perfect spouse with whom all acts were natural, even lying sick with the flu, even arguing, even being bored. And then after the one meant for you dies, what are you supposed to do, spend the rest of your existence getting over it and then make do with somebody not bad in certain respects, and work just to be working? No, screw that. What you do if horrific luck comes your way is relieve the pressure. Look at it this way, the older man with the beer and the joint said, having a taste of one and then the other, his peer pressure was no longer from the cocksuckers driving Volvo station wagons. It was from these morons here, these young goons. So simply by changing lifestyles, he was no longer a depressed member of the middle class; he was instead a respected member of the troll community.

One of the younger ones had sex with his brother and sister at the age of twelve, which probably meant that they didn't respect him much, didn't it?

Another of the younger ones had been pounded repeatedly by his father. Then in turn he started pounding on other people, most recently a man running a survivalist camp in Arkansas, who he just about beat to death. But what could those clowns do about it with all that was illegal that was going on in that dump, such as guns and molestation and what have you.

Another of the younger ones had robbed a church this morning of a large silver cross, just walking up and taking it down off a wall while people were getting crackers, acting like you owned the joint, that was the secret, with the only drawback being that you had to shave and look pretty decent.

The last of the younger ones said that his parents had been killed in a bad accident that he didn't want to talk about, and that he was currently unemployed, but that he still maintained the hope of returning to school one day soon, to junior college, as he had been told that he had some writing ability that should be developed.

Joe slipped this one fifty of the seventy bucks that he had in his pocket and told him to hang in there.

He did that when the other four went to go to the bathroom and dig up some marijuana that they had buried.

Thinking that maybe there was some good left in the world, and that the kid's presence had been a higher power's way of saying to Joe that he should just go home and work harder, he was all the way back to the rented car before it occurred to him that perhaps he had just been taken.

And by that time the fifty had in fact been divided among the men in the rocks.

CAROLYN AND DANNY
In his Range Rover, 7:00 P.M.

"Get in the right lane, Danny, you're letting me off on the next block."

"All right. Make sure somebody sees you. Notices you. Particularly in about . . . . . forty-five minutes to an hour."

"I know what an alibi is. But thanks for mentioning it."

"What's the traffic about up there?"

"It's a play."

"Yeah? What kind?"

"It's a drama. Called *Love Letters.*"

"I hate plays."

"Why's that, Danny?"

"There's very seldom any nudity. That's one. Two, they look fake. And three, you can't eat popcorn."

"Those are the best reasons I've ever heard for not liking the theater."

"Thank you very much. What's this one about, anyway?"

"Two people sit at a table in the middle of the stage and read letters that they've exchanged over the course of their lives."

"Oh come *on* with that."

"It's the truth. The story of two lives and their relationship with each another, that's what it's about, and it unfolds through some letters that began in their childhood and continued until they were elderly."

"Sounds like one big dose of elitist crud to me."

"No, it's very moving, Danny."

"Two people sitting at a table for eight hours reading bullshit letters. Nobody moves, so what could be moving?"

"It's art, Danny."

"Fart art, that's what it is. Tell me this. How old are they, the ones sitting on stage reading all the letters?"

"Oh, forties maybe. I'm guessing. I haven't seen the play in some while. Fifties perhaps."

"And they read letters written by themselves when they were *older?*"

"Yes."

"Well please, that's impossible. If they haven't *been* there yet. Am I right?"

"It's artistic license."

"Yeah well. This writer's license has expired. He needs to go back and take the test again."

"Right here at the curb is fine."

"Have a nice time at the theater while I go blow your husband's brains into ant food."

One of the things Carolyn found so galling about taking drugs was the dreary circle of co-conspirators that the habit attracted, people like sixteen-year-olds, and of course the untalented people working for their parents.

God, just think, what if she had other things in common with sixteen-year-olds, like music, speech, or nose-picking.

What if she had other things in common with the totally untalented, like the fear of being found incompetent or the urge to join a tennis club.

Sitting there in the theater watching *Love Letters*, Carolyn's mind was really going. She thought that she sort of wished that she had become obsessive about something considered more normal than drugs, something like fitness or religion or work or stupid-ass sports like her husband of fifteen years, what's-his-name; but not really, probably, because with obsessions like jumping at the health club, a person never felt herself hit the bottom. There, you jogged on the bottom or swam on the bottom. With drugs, at least you went insane; there was a noticeable need to improve.

It was just a damn shame normal people didn't take harmful drugs on a more regular basis so the company would be better.

Now where was she?

Oh yeah.

Here, this was where she stood.

Sat.

She owed money. Couldn't stand her husband, what's-his-face. Was repulsed by the attorney she had tried in his stead, Mike. Mark. Whomever. Hated her job. She had to kill him or kill herself, it was that simple. So who deserved to live more, him and his stupid games, or her, with potential?

It was a good damn thing she was married, *that* was for sure; it was a good thing he was a joke.

Carolyn got a little dizzy trying to keep it all straight and had to close her eyes and breathe deeply, couldn't attract undue attention, just had to be seen by somebody at the concession stand, her neighbor, seen and recognized.

When the people doing *Love Letters* started reading correspondence from an age period much older than what they actually and obviously were on stage, Carolyn laughed out loud and attracted a number of unpleasant stares, as the words being read at that point were related to a sorrowful event.

Carolyn whispered to the woman sitting next to her that it was impossible to read letters from a time that hadn't happened yet, from a time older than the people were.

The woman whispered back that these were the *arts,* these were *representations,* not home movies.

Carolyn said that it was starting to look to her like fart art.

"You drunk?"

"No. Not bad."

"No more beer, Joe."

"It's a done deal."

"Good. Who's in town tonight?"

"Pistons."

"Should be an easy win for the home squad. Last time I looked, the Pistons were suffering from a bad case of the whites. Listen. It's nothing personal. But I have a suggestion about your gambling trouble. You ever hear of the expression 'There's no such thing as a sick winner'?"

"No."

"My point is this, Joe. It's not the *gambling* that has you in a predicament. It's the *losing*. So once we get this situation straightened out, what you should do is handicap a game and then bet the other way. You see what I'm saying? Put the book-maker in *your* stupid-ass shoes. Determine who you think will win. Bet the other way."

"But I can't keep betting. I'm the beneficiary on no other insurance policies."

"What's the point spread on the game tonight?"

"I think the Suns are favored by around five."

"And? Who do you think is winning?"

"Jesus Christ, Tish. Do you mind if I quit something that's eating away at my self-resepct?"

"Come on, just as an experiment. Who do you like?"

"Home club, I suppose."

"So I'm betting the visitors, the Pistons plus the five points."

"No you're not."

"Sure. Five hundred."

"Well. Here's what will happen. Gambling will take control of your life. The need for action is like becoming dependent on a drug."

"Oh bullshit, Joe, that's only if you're picking like a nitwit, picking losers."

"It's a goddamn insult if you bet on the opposite of who I like, and I resent your doing it."

"Noted. Which door you want off at?"

"South. All the way around. And you're actually going to play the Pistons?"

"With confidence."

"What if my luck changes?"

"My drawers'll drop in surprise. Listen, Joe, how are you getting home?"

". . . . . After the basketball game?"

"Yeah. Sure. You're not sleeping in your seat in the arena, are you?"

". . . . . No. I don't know how I'm getting home. Cab, I guess. . . . ."

"You *usually* take cabs to and from basketball games?"

". . . . . No."

"Well, Christ, you're doing something you don't normally do, Joe. On a *very* important night. On a night that will be carefully studied by people with keys to damn jail. A night that should be routine. There'll be no record of you taking a cab *to* the basketball game. No reason why you would. So what are you going to say when somebody asks who took you to the game: the one you paid to kill your wife?"

". . . . . No . . . . . just take me to my house real quick and I'll get the car and drive back."

"No, there's not enough time. And I don't need to be seen driving you around your neighborhood. Just *say* you drove to the basketball game, all right?"

"Sure. Yeah."

"And say you parked down there on the street. No lot or receipt. Meter on the curb."

"Course. That's simple."

"All right. Hop out. Go enjoy your game. I'll go shoot your wife. When's the tip-off, anyway?"

". . . . . Eight minutes. Seven."

"That's not enough time for me to stop and make a long-distance call back home and get a bet down on the basketball game. You want to go five hundred with me, Joe? Your Suns minus the five points. I'll take Detroit."

"God Almighty. You're unbelievable. Gambling has ruined my life."

"So I hear."

"And you want to *bet* with me? You want *me* to bet?"

"Oh, yeah. I've never turned down a five-hundred-dollar bill that's easy to come by. It's a bad habit to get into, being snotty about money. No way I'm too good or too fancy to stop and pick up five hundred off the sidewalk."

". . . . . I'm not *that* bad a picker."

"Sure you are. I could beat you easy. And I'm a girl. Want to bet?"

"All right. Okay. You've got a big mouth. I'll take the Suns minus five points. Good-bye. . . . ."

"Hey . . . . ."

". . . . . Yeah."

"How are you actually getting home, for God's sake?"

"Oh . . . . . that. Don't know. . . . ."

"How far is it?"

"Three miles. Three and a half."

"Walk. It's good exercise, everybody knows that. And say you walked to and from the game."

The man Danny was going to shoot for thirty thousand dollars was to have been sitting in a television room watching a basketball game on a new picture-in-a-picture set; sex and sports all at once, not bad, Danny thought—why ever go outside again.

He had a simple sketch of the house with roughly drawn squares representing the rooms and X's standing for the doors. It had been drawn by the woman of the house, the one who was fixing to become the *person* of the house, the only one left.

The television room was toward the front of the dwelling. Good, since Danny was coming in through the back door with a key. The farther away from the victim the better. And the television room was without windows. Good again, because Danny didn't want anybody having the opportunity to jump through any glass and on outside.

It was a simple layout to comprehend, even in the near darkness. You went in through a back door, which had a wood frame and a big glass center, to the kitchen; through the kitchen to a hallway, up the hallway to the television room; you shot the poor unsuspecting sports-loving sap in the head, you took a few valuables, you left.

Now, going into the kitchen, that was *not* so good, because basketball games had lots of commercials in them and the kitchen was a popular place to go during such an occasion, there, or to the toilet, one of which was just off the television room.

So Danny was ready should somebody walk suddenly into the kitchen as he was in the process of entering the home, and a pretty nice one it was, too, as far as he could see in the reflection of a light coming from up front. The kitchen had a lot of cool-colored tile on the floor and counters, and blue cabinets, a pretty happy-looking place, all around.

After opening the back door and stepping silently into the

kitchen, Danny had his gun out and aimed at the door leading to the rest of the house. If somebody came through that doorway, and was of an adult size, he would shoot them, period, hello-good-bye, next basket case. Somebody child-sized, he'd try extremely hard not to shoot. Killing a kid, who needed that.

Danny had a feeling that interested him a great deal as he closed the rear door and looked back toward the main part of the house.

It was almost like a revelation.

An awakening, almost, perhaps.

He wanted to live.

Now could you beat that.

He almost tripped over the feeling, no kidding; it startled him and he stopped walking for a few seconds and stood listening for basketball sounds coming off a television.

Usually during dangerous work he felt like, well, fuck it, if I die, I die. Usually his dangerous work came after depressing separations from women he loved, so that was probably it—he was too sad or pissed off to pay much attention to life.

So now all of a sudden why did he feel like he wanted to live?

Maybe it had something to do with not being as young as he used to be.

Weird.

And kind of awe-inspiring.

Standing there in the middle of the kitchen belonging to some guy he was going to put down for thirty thousand in cash, Danny started thinking about pink sunrises and orange sunsets, about Super Bowls and breasts without surgical padding, about black cocker spaniels and bowls of chili; well, maybe not pink sunrises because he was seldom up that early, but all the rest.

Good God Almighty, Danny thought, have I just had something similar to a religious experience?

He considered that briefly.

Stopped breathing.

Looked around for some white light flashes, angels, the

bearded face of Jesus come to love him and inform him of a greater good.

Didn't see a damn thing, though.

So that wasn't it.

He simply didn't want this life to end here in a pool of blood on this kitchen floor.

Some maturity had to have set in, who knew?

Wanting to live, maybe it meant something very good had a chance to enter his life, a big love, a gorgeous mute, could be.

And with wanting to live came fear.

So Danny moved quieter and slower than he ever had, passing through the kitchen using one step every ten or so seconds, hearing clocks tick in other rooms, hearing caged birds chirp from a place to his left.

But there was no basketball game playing in the television room. There was nothing playing. The television room was empty, the set was off. Danny stood in the hallway for a full minute, making sure it was quiet in there. Then he stepped inside and looked around, walking first to the television set and feeling its top and back. It was cool, meaning it hadn't been on recently, didn't it? It seemed like he had seen somebody feeling tubes in a movie. But all the technology, hell, what tubes, there were wires.

Next, not wanting to be neurotic, but also wishing to stay on the live side, he inspected the cushions on the leather chair, finding them level and unwrinkled, suggesting nobody had been seated there recently; then he worked his way forward through the house, going through all the closets in case somebody with a sharp hatchet waited in one, finding nobody.

But there was a car in the garage located off the kitchen, a car cold like the television.

Well bullshit, Danny thought, this is not orderly as planned; this is quiet chaos.

He went back into the kitchen and sat down at the table and put his gun on it and thought about what he should do now.

He didn't like this at all and was liking it less every five seconds, then every two.

You got ready for something in a certain way, and if it happened otherwise, you could be surprised, caught unaware, and then find yourself in something horrific like a shoot-out as a result, ducking behind furniture and firing or some dumb-ass thing like that.

No, one way, that was the only way this should have gone.

Oh sure, he could wait.

But what if seven people came in the front door?

He didn't wait.

He went out the back way, locking the door behind himself with the key, pissed off.

JOE'S ANSWERING MACHINE
On the desk in the television room, 10:15 P.M.

"Hi. You've reached five-five-five, three-six-four-five. Calls from car phones aren't accepted, sorry. . . . . (beep) . . . . ."

". . . . . Joe? . . . . This is, uh, hi, this is Tish. . . . . It's a little after ten and, uh, listen, why don't you give me a call just as soon as you get a chance. It's important, the number is five-five-five, fifty-four-hundred. . . . ."

Danny went to the first convenience store he could find and called Carolyn's work number on one of the outside pay phones.

Lord, lord, banks of pay phones outside convenience stores, there should have been a city ordinance against these filthy lie-producing things, particularly late on a Friday night.

Plastic gloves should have been dispensed from a machine; where was a large can of Lysol when you needed it?

The only pay phone open was the second from the left of a group of four, so Danny made a sour face and went to use it, to call Carolyn, stepping over a puddle of something brown and lumpy—what, he didn't want to know.

The person on the pay phone left of Danny was drinking a can of beer and crying into the receiver and saying he would never again do whatever he had done; then he held that pay phone out to Danny and said here, tell her I'm not drinking.

Danny said fuck you, get that thing away from me, telling the man that he had problems of his own, he wasn't here to practice psychotherapy.

Oh yeah? the guy said. He quit crying and asked Danny if he wanted to fight.

Danny asked the lunatic to his left if he wanted to *die* and turned to face the other way.

The guy on that pay phone was telling somebody he had to work late, then he waved to a young woman sitting in the middle of the front seat of a rickety pickup truck.

Then he said no, of course not, he wasn't out screwing around again, he wasn't with anybody, he was working the late shift on the line and was taking a break now.

He waved again to the one in the truck and she blew him a kiss.

The one he was talking to on the phone must have been an ugly mother because the one in the middle of the front seat of the pickup was no bargain, as she had a round piglike face and a large Roman-looking nose to go with it.

The one using the pay phone on the far right end was telling somebody he was going to kill himself.

Good, Danny thought, wishing for a little peace and quiet.

The guy to Danny's left said that this was your lucky day, friend; the one thing he had promised his wife was that he would never fight again.

The one to Danny's right said into his receiver that he swore to God he was not sneaking around with a beautiful woman, winning that one on a technicality.

The one on the far right end said that if whomever he was talking to didn't try to talk him out of killing himself, then he'd *really* fucking kill himself.

Danny started to hand the guy a gun.

Nobody answered the first time, but since there were some liars and cheats and cowards and drunks and morons parked nearby and waiting for a pay phone to open up, Danny stayed with it, calling Carolyn's office number over and over, finally getting an answer on about the fourth minute of trying.

Having to be ready to defend himself against his fellow pay-phone users took some of the edge off Danny's anger. But he was still very upset.

Carolyn had just run into her office from the play and was breathless on that account, as well as being jittery from the tension caused by the call and the news Danny had to relate.

She wanted to know if it was over, how it had happened, she wanted to know everything.

Everything was goddamn *nothing*, Danny said. He wasn't there, her husband. . . . .

Not there? *Not there?* What did he mean, not there?

Danny said that he meant that there was nobody in the miserable, stinking, Yuppie Estates goddamn house, *that* was what he meant by nothing. He meant nobody was there and nothing happened. And he told her to quit interrupting, babbling, gasping, and irritating him.

He was yelling so she got quiet.

He said he looked everywhere. The television wasn't on. He waited twenty minutes. So here he was. On edge. Mentally prepared. Wound up tight. Using a pay phone next to some white, no, *green* trash drunk to the gills.

Somebody to the right resented that remark, not that Danny cared.

Carolyn asked him if he had gone to the proper house and then quickly apologized. He was supposed to have been there, Joe was. He *had* to have been there because sports and nude women were on the air.

Yeah well, Danny told her, that and a dollar wouldn't get you much of anything.

Carolyn asked for a number where Danny could be reached. She said she'd try to find out what had happened and get right back to him.

Danny replied that he couldn't be reached at any number, as

it was approaching midnight on a Friday and there were liars on all sides of him waiting to spread their insanity here at the convenience-store phone bank.

Two people didn't care for that remark, one on each side of Danny.

He looked one way and then the other and told them that he didn't care for their *lives*.

Carolyn then asked Danny to please give her a few minutes and call her back.

He said he'd try.

And then he said it would cost her.

JOE'S ANSWERING MACHINE
On a desk in the television room, five minutes after midnight

"Hi. You've reached five-five-five, three-six-four-five. Calls from car phones aren't accepted, sorry . . . . . . (beep). . . . ."

"Uh, yeah, Joe, it's me again, Tish, uh. . . . ."

". . . . . *Wait,* hell, I'm here, I just ran in the front door. Don't hang up. Let me shut this machine off . . . . you still there, Tish?"

"Yes."

"How'd it go? Oh my God. Is it over? Jesus. Let me sit down and . . . . ."

"No, it's not over."

". . . . What did you say? It's *not* over? What is it then?"

"It's, uh, in suspended animation. She wasn't there. She wasn't in her office."

"*What?* Come on . . . . . are you sure?"

"About as sure as the security guard who said she left the office at about a quarter after seven. Turned the lights off. Locked her office door."

"Oh my *God.* . . . . Oh, hell. . . . . I don't know if I could do *this* again. I was mentally prepared for it to happen. . . . ."

"Listen Joe, right now your emotional well-being isn't my primary concern. Your ability to get things straight *is* . . . . ."

"She was supposed to be there, she said she would be

there . . . . . hang on a second. I'm getting beeped on call-waiting, another call is coming in, I'll be right back. . . . . Yeah, hello?"

". . . . . *Joe?*"

". . . . . *Carolyn?*"

"Joe, where the hell have you *been?*"

"Where have *I* been? I've been to a damn basketball game. Where have *you* been? And how do you know I've been anywhere? There were no messages on the answering machine."

"I . . . . . stopped by."

"I thought you were going to work late at your goddamn office, Carolyn. I called you . . . . . three times."

"I wasn't getting anywhere. I . . . . . went to a play."

"I swear to *Christ,* Carolyn, I just don't know why you don't do what you say."

"Why are you so upset about my going to a play, anyway?"

"I'm not upset."

"Well, you're yelling."

"No I'm not, Carolyn."

"Now you're not."

"Why would you care if I went to a basketball game?"

"Oh . . . . . I just wanted to . . . . . talk."

"Well, here I am. Back home. Talk."

"Now I need to work, Joe, I'm way behind on a couple of projects due Monday."

"All right. You going to . . . . . be there a while, Carolyn?"

"Yeah Joe, afraid so. Bent over the desk. What about you? What are you going to do?"

"Well, Carolyn, midnight, I'm sitting here in my boxer shorts. That sort of limits my options to what's inside the house. I'm going to bed."

"All right, Joe. Well. See you later."

"Good luck on your work projects, Carolyn."

"Thanks, Joe."

"There's no rush getting home. I'll just . . . . . put in a movie."

"Good. Get some rest. You seem very stressed out lately.

Relax. How about putting on your new earphones and listening to some music instead of watching a movie."

"Doesn't sound bad. And you just take your time there at work."

"Will do. How was the basketball game?"

"Pretty sorry. The stupid home team lost outright to a team of pale faces."

"I'm sorry."

"How was the play, Carolyn?"

"So-so."

"What was it?"

"*Love Letters.*"

"No kidding. Remember when we saw that in Los Angeles?"

"Now don't start any of that sentimental stuff with me, Joe."

"Why would I do that?"

"Don't know. Can't say. Maybe you feel guilty about something. But I have to go, Joe."

"All right."

"..... Wait."

"..... Yeah, Carolyn?"

".......... Nothing."

".......... Fine."

"Good-bye."

".........Yeah....."

....

".......... Hello, Tish, you still there?"

"Still here."

"She's back at work. At the office. That was her just then on the other line. She went to a play. She said she was going to work late at her office, by herself. For quite a while."

"All right."

"So go *get* her."

"Don't worry about me. Just take care of your stuff. Be somewhere in forty minutes. Make it thirty."

"Why?"

"Alibi."

". . . . . Oh yeah."

"If I had a hundred for every time you said *oh yeah.* By the way, bring me the half a thousand you lost on the basketball game."

Danny had one of the lying, cheating convenience-store pay phone–using motherfuckers in a headlock and was squeezing him tight as he called Carolyn once more, *real* tight.

The one he had in a headlock had come to the bank of pay phones to call some woman and tell her that he had cancer. Like who had run the test and had given him the results at this hour—the convenience store clerk? Cancer. Man, had *this* guy been through the excuses for abhorrent behavior. His excuse history probably looked something like this: car trouble, flu, sick relative, sick dog, dead dog, dead relative, had to work late, got fired, car wreck, cancer.

The woman he had called to explain away his absence as a result of cancer wasn't having any part of it. So the guy at the pay phone held the receiver out to Danny and said here, you tell her how bad sick I am.

He reeked of fruit-flavored alcohol, peach vodka, something cheap and nasty like that.

Danny was as diplomatic as was possible under the circumstances and the hour, telling the man who was seven hours late with somebody that he wasn't telling anybody anything, he was just going to use the pay phone, that was it, no medical update, no probing of the body, no more sloppy drunken babble.

The man in trouble with the woman said that you are so going to tell her what I want you to, and he touched a long and dirty finger to Danny's chest.

It was at this point when Danny put the man in a headlock, quickly wrapping his left forearm around the guy's temples and yanking him down to waist level and whacking him hard on top of the head with the pay-phone receiver, five times, cracking the plastic on about the third whack.

Goddamn, the man getting whacked repeatedly yelled.

Danny grabbed the receiver left dangling by the man in the headlock and told the woman he had been talking to that this twerp didn't have cancer of anything except perhaps the imagination, and that he wasn't alone, there was a drunk-looking teenager-type female with big ears in the front seat of his truck.

The other liars at the phone bank didn't like what was going on and covered their receivers and said come on man, knock it off, the whacking with the receiver and the yelling wasn't doing their own stories any good at all.

So Danny turned his attention back to his phone and the number he had just dialed, Carolyn's, again. He didn't want three more drunk liars jumping him. Two, fine; three, he'd pass—one of three could get in a lucky slash across his face.

Carolyn was on the line and had heard what had happened. She apologized for the inconvenience of his having to call her back.

He said *inconvenience* didn't do the near riot justice.

It was like apologizing to the Japanese for the inconvenience of the bomb.

This was a nightmare.

For which Carolyn quickly apologized.

But she said she had some important news.

He was back home, her husband was, and he sounded tired, Joe did, wasn't that good, wasn't that *great*. And, better than watching a basketball game in the television room, he was now watching a movie in bed. So Danny could waltz over and take him right on down. She didn't say *waltz* but she thought it. Because putting him away now sounded so simple. So she said go over there and get him.

Danny replied that this would cost three thousand more, no, four, and Carolyn said okay, okay, before he went any higher.

JOE AND CAROLYN
Their favorite restaurant, Blanche's, one in the morning

"*Joe!*"

"My God, Carolyn, *what are you doing here?*"

"Joe. Listen to me. Please *leave.*"

"What?"

"Go *home.*"

"I thought you said you were working, Carolyn. *Again.*"

"Now I mean it, Joe. If I *ever* meant anything to you, anything at all, I want you to turn around and leave this restaurant and go home right this instant and go to goddamn bed."

"This is absolutely amazing. . . . ."

"What are you *doing?* . . . . ."

"Sitting the hell down, Carolyn, before I tip over. . . . ."

"At *my* table? . . . . ."

"I'm not sitting on the floor. . . . . Waiter, over here, that's right, listen, I need a bottle of your quickest whiskey. . . . ."

"*Joe!*"

"*Carolyn!*"

"Okay, Joe, damn it, keep your voice down. I have something very important to ask you."

"Go ahead."

"Are you going home or not?"

"No."

"*No?*"

"No."

"You're the most unbelievable person I've ever met."

"Are you going back to work?"

"*No.*"

"Ah, boy."

"Why do you care if I go back to work, anyway? Are you *meeting* somebody here?"

"No Carolyn. Christ. Hell. Jesus."

"Then why do you care if I go back to work?"

"Why do *I* care?"

"Yes. Tell me."

"I *don't* care."

"Then be quiet about it. Quit harping, am I going to work, am I going to work."

"All right."

"And you're not going home?"

"I'll go home with *you,* Carolyn, since you're not working."

"You will?"

"Yes. We will. Why wouldn't we go home together?"

"I don't know, Joe. For sweet Jesus' sake high in heaven. No reason whatsoever, I guess."

"So . . . . ."

"God . . . . ."

"Man . . . . ."

"Well . . . . ."

"I have an idea, Carolyn."

"What is it, Joe?"

"Since nobody is leaving . . . . ."

"No . . . . ."

"Let's start this conversation over."

"All right. I guess. Whatever."

"Okay. Ready, Carolyn?"

"Sure. Good God."

"What's wrong?"

"Nothing."

". . . . . Hi, Carolyn."

". . . . . Hello, Joe."

"So how was the . . . ."

"Play, Joe. I went to a play."

"How was the play?"

"Oh. A little dated, actually."

"How's that?"

"It was, I don't know, too nice . . . . . too sweet. Too pleasant. Too honest. Says a lot for the times, doesn't it, good and pure and true seeming dated."

"Yeah."

"How was your game?"

"It smelled."

"The pageantry?"

"Sucked."

"The comradeship?"

"Double suck."

"I'm sorry."

"How come you came here, Carolyn?"

"Piece of pie, Joe. Chocolate icebox. Yourself?"

"Same. Remember the first time we came here, Carolyn?"

"Sure do, Joe."

"Sat over there in the corner."

"Yep."

"Remember what you did with your foot?"

"Yeah I remember. It's not the kind of thing I was in the habit of doing. Placing it between your legs and rubbing."

"I was talking about when you sprained your ankle."

"Aren't you funny."

"I've been funnier."

"Who our age hasn't, Joe."

"Carolyn?"

"Yeah, Joe, what is it?"

"You look nice."

"Yeah? Where?"

"Basically everywhere except your fists, Carolyn. You ought to unmake them and stay a while."

Carolyn suddenly opened her purse and had Joe lean over, and then she showed him what was in a little bag inside.

It was cocaine, a bunch of it.

Tears came from her eyes with no change of expression. Like a valve had been opened. She smiled as though the tears had relieved some pressure.

She said it was eating her up and she couldn't stand it anymore. Sitting here in this charming little piece of shit restaurant where they had come to grin and have decaf coffee and chocolate icebox pie after they had screwed each other silly fifteen years ago, it reminded her of normalcy; she couldn't keep her sad secret anymore.

She had been using cocaine for a year, heavier with each month.

She had also been selling it to some of her friends, buying it here, selling it there, and she had run up a pretty good-sized tab that was pending; she owed around eleven thousand dollars. That was because she had used some of what she was going to sell. Damn it.

She said she was embarrassed.

She said she felt weak and common.

But she said that she also felt good for having told him. She couldn't remember the last reasonably important thing that she had shared with him. That was probably part of what was wrong with their relationship, wasn't it, treating each other like neighbors instead of friends and lovers.

So that was that. Here take it, she said, putting the bag of cocaine on the table in their favorite restaurant. Not wanting to go to jail on what could have been an upbeat note, Joe quickly put a napkin over the drugs.

Carolyn smiled in such a genuine way that Joe had to smile back; it was like she had just told a good, clean joke.

And it continued to seem as though they had just met, with Carolyn's hand feeling friendly and even just a little bit sensual under Joe's touch.

So she was out from under it, praise be. She was going to a rehab center just as soon as she could find one that would have her. No more easy ways out. No more acting. No more lies. The money she owed to the person who sold her drugs, well, he'd just have to be patient, she'd pay it out, get another job, something good-spirited like that.

She told Joe that she was really sorry.

He said that he had known she was using cocaine, had known it for a couple of months. Carolyn's dealer had called him about the debt when it reached seventy-five hundred dollars. Joe had found the whole thing to be pretty disgusting, pretty average. He figured her habit would get worse and worse and worse until she got so desperate she either killed herself or went stealing. But she hadn't been the only one in the house going off three-quarters baked.

He told her about his compulsive gambling habit that had him eighteen thousand dollars in debt, a sum that caused Carolyn to frown and whistle and feel just a little silly about having gotten so emotional about being only *eleven* grand in arrears.

Joe said that the risk that came with gambling was his drug— betting money on sporting events was his relief from the rigors of everyday life, which, like all artificial stimulants, came with a stiff price tag.

But just as she was finished with her habit, so too was he done with his, he was going to call Gamblers Anonymous and start going to meetings and begin some personal counseling on the side, as well.

And he could see what she meant about being out from under a suffocating shroud of guilt and fear.

He didn't want to sound sappy or anything, but at the moment he was feeling in a slightly reborn mood.

Carolyn said that she had known about his gambling, she had

gone through his desk and had seen all the numbers, and of course she had watched him meld into the wavelengths coming from the television screen for dozens of hours in a single sitting.

She just hadn't known how terrible a gambler he was, though, eighteen grand, *wow*, that smelled.

Her best guess about what would happen was he'd get so far in debt that one day men without remorse would cut open some part of his body, or that he'd just up and take off and leave her to explain to the stiffed gamblers how much the Persian rugs were worth as they rolled and bound them and carried them off, along with Carolyn's jewelry.

First he told her about having been with the recent college graduate from the school of journalism, and then she quickly informed him of her attorney; and they solemnly nodded at each other as if there had been no other way it had could have happened. Then their eyes moistened and they smiled some forgiveness at each other.

So after having explained the worst of what had been hidden under the dark side of their brains, they sat grinning outright at each other, like they were glad to have met for the first time.

And they were so pleased with their sharing and caring and confessing that they went and did it in a stall in the men's room with Joe sitting on the stool and Carolyn facing the same direction and lowering herself gently onto his lap at first, the back side of her dress draped over the top of her head, and the front side held in her teeth so nobody could see anything under the door.

It was wildly exciting and it was all they could do to keep from making noises that would lead to their being discovered.

Joe tried to help by putting his right palm around Carolyn's mouth so she could scream into that, but it didn't work; she bit him bloody and then spat some of it out on the stall wall.

They willed themselves quiet as Carolyn braced herself by placing her hands on both sides of the stall and then sliding up and down on his best feature at the moment ten times, twenty, thirty, while he put his hands on her hips and guided her and basically sat there and grinned and bore it.

Carolyn had a good curve to her hips.

Joe enjoyed holding onto them.

He whispered into Carolyn's right ear that he had it all figured out here. What he would do was hold very tight to her hips so she wouldn't fly into the air when he came, and she thought oh, sure, big shot, but could only manage to whisper back something that came out garbled.

Once they were finished taking care of each other, and what a new and thoughtful thing that was for him to do, to hang in and up there a while longer, they took a couple of moments to catch their breath and then they walked right on out the men's room like they belonged there because Carolyn was not about to apologize for being a healthy heterosexual woman in love with her own husband.

They returned to their table and ordered wine but not too much because gamblers and dope-takers weren't exactly known for their abilities to deal with temptations similar in nature to their own core problems.

They held hands and appeared to be enjoying their company so much that the waiter asked if it was an anniversary. Joe said yeah it was and looked at his watch. It was their happy two-hour anniversary.

The waiter smiled and said it was a start.

After that, they talked about important things like boundaries. Actually, Carolyn talked about boundaries and Joe paid polite and thorough attention and nodded at the critical spots. Carolyn said she was well aware that Joe didn't put too much faith in what he considered to be trendy therapy. He had once said that he was going to count her self-help books, which numbered 103, and take out an advertisement in the newspaper telling people how many she had. But boundaries were extremely important to Carolyn, as they insured privacy and individuality and helped prevent boredom from infiltrating a relationship. She would have her boundaries, her complete and total control over herself, or there was no need in going on with anything. Except perhaps one more incident of sex.

Joe said he would learn to understand and honor her boundaries.

Carolyn said, now, she *meant* it.

Joe raised a knife and asked what she wanted from him, a little finger?

She grinned and said no, all she wanted was a thoughtful partner.

Joe didn't know what in the hell he could do that wouldn't detract from the passion Carolyn felt about such relationship aids as boundaries, so he just sat there.

While on the subject of therapy, Carolyn said she wanted them to go to codependency meetings and to counseling and to church and maybe even to school of some kind.

Joe said great, and they shook on it.

They talked about traveling to some places where they could learn something about the human condition as well as see something new and inspiring, like how about *Nepal,* Carolyn said, and Joe replied uh, yeah, sure, why not.

Improvement, that would be the watchword of the rest of their time together.

They talked about what they liked about each other and what they didn't like.

They could never forget what had brought them back together and had given them this opportunity for some well-worn happiness, and that was an honest openness.

Some of the things Carolyn couldn't stand about Joe were his jealousy, his selfishness, and his extremely offensive attitudes, or at least reactions, toward lesbians.

Carolyn had many lesbian friends.

Joe called them the sexually special.

And Carolyn said that kind of thing had to stop right now.

Joe smiled and nodded and said that it was just sometimes difficult for heterosexual males not to tease lesbians.

He never minded when lesbians teased him.

But if it meant a lot to Carolyn, he would study the subject of lesbianism and come to understand the appeal of licking on one who had the same stuff as you did. Because understanding was the first step toward respectful coexistence.

Carolyn also had many gay men friends.

She would continue to welcome gays and lesbians into her home and wanted them treated with the utmost respect.

Joe said ignorance would not stop him, and at this time next year he would be having some lesbians over for supper.

Carolyn wondered if he were being a smart-ass, but gave him the benefit of any doubt in this, the second hour of their new lives together.

Some of the things she liked about him were his sense of humor, his tenderness and thoughtfulness during sex, and his wild streak of originality.

Things Joe liked about Carolyn were her open-mindedness, her nicely tapered legs, her forgiving nature, her strong sense of spirituality, and her tuna casserole.

Things he could do without was a tendency of hers to move quickly toward most things fashionable and current, like popular books, films, and self-help theories, and the creative frustration she seemed to feel because he wrote and she didn't.

They agreed to discuss further all of their likes and dislikes with each other at a weekly family meeting.

Throughout the big time at their favorite restaurant, they spoke excitedly about being rehabilitated from what had turned their respective lives into walking case histories for shrinks and, almost, detectives; and while they were frightened about how difficult the treatment and healing would be, they were joyful about having a loving partner at their side.

They held hands on and off and leaned over the table and kissed a half a dozen times.

They went from wine to decaffeinated coffee.

Carolyn said she wanted to have sex some more.

Joe said she'd get no argument from him.

She said that she had a couple of things to pick up at her office and then she'd be right home. . . . .

. . . . . And Joe told her to *wait* with such suddenness and firmness that she jumped and jerked her hand back and sloshed some coffee out of her cup.

She had started to get up, but sat back down.

Joe sighed, rubbed his eyes.

The back of his neck.

Said he had something important to say, something *else* important.

But first he needed to get some air out front.

Said he'd be right back.

So he went outside and paced back and forth on the sidewalk in front of their favorite restaurant and decided the only way to get to it was directly and succinctly and with kindness and compassion.

JOE AND CAROLYN
Still at their favorite restaurant, same table, at closing time

"Don't go to your office, Carolyn."

"I have to go to my office, Joe. I told you, I need to bring a report home."

"You can't go to your office."

"Yes I can. What in the hell are you talking about, anyway. . . . ."

"No, you goddamn *cannot* go to your office. Do you hear what I'm saying?"

"I hear what you're *shouting*. And I don't like it. It brings back bad memories of your former horse's-ass self."

"Shouting is the only way I can be understood."

"Oh what a lovely conclusion to the evening."

"It's better than you think, Carolyn."

"So why are you saying, why are you *ordering* me not to go to my office? For five minutes. To pick up a folder."

"I'll tell you. Please lean over the table."

"Why?"

"So I can speak softly."

"You don't want strangers hearing you boss me around?"

"Yes. . . . ."

"*Trying* to boss me around . . . . ."

"Okay, okay. . . . ."

"All right, Joe. There. I'm over the table. Tell me softly why I can't go by my place of business for *twenty seconds.*"

"Because somebody is waiting there to kill you."

. . . .

. . . .

". . . . . What did you just say?"

"Somebody's waiting at your office to murder you. Shoot you. I think."

"Come on, Joe. This isn't clever. Watch it, now. . . . ."

"It's true. God as my witness."

"Well, it better *not* be."

"Well Carolyn, you're just going to have to be outraged because it is a fact. Because I hired her. *Okay?*"

". . . . . You? . . . . ."

"Yeah."

"Hired somebody to *kill* me?"

"Correct."

"*Me?* The one you just said all those wonderful things about?"

"Carolyn, good God, I hired the woman to kill you *long* before we got back together, you know that, come on, we *just* got back together."

"Let me see if I have this arranged straight in my mind. *You* hired somebody to kill *me* . . . . . *tonight* . . . . . at my *office?*"

"Yes. And please keep your voice down."

"Why you no-good cocksucking son of a bitch. . . . ."

"Now wait just one minute. . . . ."

"Who?"

". . . . . because I *am* telling you not to go to your office . . . . ."

"*Who,* Joe?"

"Did I hire?"

"Yes."

"A woman."

"What woman?"

"I don't know exactly what woman. Tish. That's what she said her name was. Big wig, goofy glasses ....."

"You chicken. You hired a *yuppie* to kill me?"

"I don't know what she is. The one I owed, the one I owe, the bookmaker, he got her for me. She's from somewhere else."

"Why are you having me killed, Joe?"

"I appreciate your soft tone here, Carolyn. It encourages open communication and honesty. *Was* having you killed, Carolyn, *was.*"

"I'm so mad at you, so thoroughly disgusted and sickened, I'm thinking about throwing my glass of water right at your face."

"Now the waiter is looking, Carolyn. We don't want the police coming, I'll promise you that."

"All right. Deep breath. I'm fine. Tell me. Why do you want me dead?"

"*Did* want you dead ....."

"*Did, goddamn it* ....."

"Okay, easy now. Well, Carolyn, it seemed like the thing to do at the time. I was, I *am*, in very serious debt. You were using drugs. The insurance money looked pretty good. I was sick. Unbalanced. Desperate. Incoherent, almost. I panicked. In my mind, it seemed like you or me; it was precisely that simple."

"..... This is the lowest point of any life we had together. Worse than drugs. Worse than gambling."

"No it's not. It's a speed bump. Good God, you can't punish me for being honest with you. ....."

"Call her, Joe. Call it off."

"Well ....."

"Well *what?*"

"Calling her. I don't know. Actually I can't call her, Carolyn. I told you, she's from out of town. She has no phone in her rented car. She's ..... simply waiting at your office to kill you. I'm afraid at the moment we're ..... where we are."

"We're fucking where we *are*, is that what you're looking me in the eye and saying? ....."

"Yes. . . . ."

"A killer is looking for me and *we're where we are?*"

"I simply thought it was more optimistic than anything else I might say."

"Oh, Jesus. . . . .Wait, I have an idea, Joe."

"What, sweetheart?"

"You could write her. Drop her a card. Say please don't shoot my wife."

"Carolyn, easy, honey. . . . ."

"I'd like to turn this table over on top of you and jump up and down on it."

"With all due respect, I wouldn't recommend it."

"So just what in the hell am I supposed to do *now?*"

"Well. It's not that complicated. Not that dangerous. Why don't you go to a motel somewhere and call me. When Tish doesn't find you at the office, she'll check in with me."

"Don't ever call her *Tish* again in my presence."

"She said it was her name, Carolyn."

"I don't care what she said her name was. Don't call somebody trying to shoot me by her *first name.*"

"All right."

"So now you'll be going . . . . . where the hell, Joe?"

"Home, baby. To wait for her call. Your call."

"The insurance money sounding better to you, Joe? You sorry we got back together?"

". . . . . No."

"Boy, *that* pisses me off. You didn't answer right away."

"Yes I did, Carolyn, I was swallowing when you asked the question and I didn't want to choke."

"I'm afraid to go out that door, Joe. Somebody could be waiting to kill me."

"Oh, I seriously doubt that. She's at your office. Outside your office. You know, somewhere around it."

"Maybe she *was* at my office."

"She'd have no reason to leave yet. No reason to look here."

"You didn't mention this restaurant as a favorite place of mine?"

"I . . . . . don't think so. I might have. Once. Briefly if at all."

"Okay Joe, you no-good son of a gun, I'm getting out of here. Out of this neighborhood. I'll call you when I'm all snuggled in to that sorry little motel by the airport."

Joe thought:

Oh great, here I am getting my life turned around for the better and my relationship with my wife is going more pleasantly than it has in years, maybe ever, and now this.

Now I'm being strangled.

He had driven home and had stopped his car in the driveway without putting it in the garage and was walking toward the front door to go inside and wait for Tish to call so he could tell her not to kill his wife and hope to get off for a couple of thousand dollars lost in trouble money, when somebody stepped from behind a large boxwood bush covered with thick green leaves and got him around the neck and started choking from the rear.

Joe was usually reasonably cautious about looking all ways before going anywhere at night, but he had plenty on his mind this evening and was simply walking and not paying attention. Stop wife from being killed. Figure way to pay bookmaker. Turn life around. Be supportive of former druggie wife. Don't gamble. Watch for strangler in bushes—that was the *last* thing on his mind.

Somebody got him from behind, a male obviously, going by the tough muscle in the forearm. Somebody got Joe by placing his neck in the crook of his left arm and by squeezing.

As he squeezed he called Joe by name and said don't even think about resisting, then he tapped the back of Joe's skull with something hard that he said was a loaded pistol.

Understand?

Joe nodded that hell yeah, he understood. Some of it. And what he didn't understand, he'd pretend to.

The man who had him shoved him toward the front steps of the porch and told him to sit there and relax so they could have a talk.

The one who had been behind the boxwood bush wore glasses that were darkly tinted, a crooked reddish wig, and a ball cap. He had some whiskers on his face, real ones, about a quarter of an inch in length.

So Joe went to the front steps and sat down and folded his hands in front of him.

The guy who had caught and then released him like a small trout put his pistol away and came to the porch and sat beside Joe, cautioning him once more not to fuck around.

Joe raised his right hand as though testifying in a court of law and said he wouldn't fuck around, while wondering if the man next to him there on the top step had the wrong address, the wrong party; but no, he had called Joe by name, hadn't he.

They sat there, on the top step, without speaking, for between thirty seconds and a minute. Still somewhat afraid for his life, it seemed longer to Joe. But he watched the second hand creep around on his watch. As they sat, the telephone inside Joe's house rang and was answered by the machine. Then it rang again and was answered again. And a third time.

The man beside Joe said that his name was Danny.

Joe nodded, while wondering if he should perhaps try to:

1. Slip his two-thousand-dollar watch off his wrist and slide it into some shrubbery by the side of the front porch. Or:

2. Bring his left elbow up and back suddenly, catching this character on the point of his chin, and shattering it, as his teeth smashed together and cut off half his tongue. Or:

3. Sit still.

He picked 3; it took him one second to decide.

The telephone inside the house rang again and was answered once more by the machine.

Danny asked what was this, anyway, Grand Central?

Joe hadn't known that Grand Central got a lot of telephone

calls, but smiled apologetically at the slightly off-center comparison anyhow.

Danny put his thoughts together for another minute or so and then proclaimed:

It was looking like a man thing to him.

Ah Jesus, it probably went back to his father, but then, what didn't, you know? Father. Lack of a father. One of the two, it was a cornerstone of adult life. God*damn*, if Danny would have known how important a good father was then, he'd have beaten the hell out of his old man and asked him to straighten up. But as it was, he just let the overweight drunk punch on him, it was his one moment of remote importance, you know? Knocking down a kid, that was the one thing he thought he could do with any degree of skill, but in actuality it was the kid letting him have a good minute, the old sot piece of crap, hell, Danny would put his arms in front of his face and he would roll himself into a ball like before he was born, and his father hardly even hurt him except for a lucky glancing shot. God only knew what might have happened had Danny stood up to his father and said, okay, all right, you worthless bunch of hangover scars, no more. If Danny had put down his father and stomped the cheap booze out of him, the old man would have had no reason to live, right? And nobody wants his father, however big a flab-ass bully, to take his life so . . .

Joe excused himself politely and asked what might be the best way to put forward a question or two at some point, and Danny said you shouldn't interrupt somebody pouring out his soul to you. . . .

. . . So Joe shut up tight . . .

. . . and Danny said the male sensation was the one thing they couldn't take away from you. They could take away your money and they could take away your marijuana and they could take away your house and they could take away your motivation and they could take away your freedom and they could even take away your dog, but one thing they could never take away was your *maleness,* your brotherly spirit, your rugged individuality and fierce yet loyal and caring nature, by Christ. . . .

Joe mumbled damn right while swallowing hard . . .

. . . as Danny was going on down his own private road.

See, Danny said, it went like this. She reminded him of Dee Dee, the love of his life and his hereafter, who just up and left one morning, using as a feeble excuse the lame angle that she was pretty scared of him so just think how scared that made her of his *enemies,* all five hundred of them. She had kind of a hard edge to her, Dee Dee did, when it came to matters of contemporary male-female relations, so she called it. Several times Dee Dee threatened to sue him for breach of promise, for example, for saying that he'd buy her things like a LeBaron convertible and then never doing it. Threats so aroused a sense of male anger in him that he wanted to go out and fuck six of Dee Dee's best friends, but only three of them would go for it. And that other woman had a pretty nasty side to her, too, the one who hired Danny to kill Joe did, setting it up to happen in the front of the house there in the television room with a pro basketball game going on, not a touch of remorse evident, not the slightest mention of any good times together, just the hard-line approach: Take your gun and unlock the back door and proceed quietly up the hallway off the kitchen to the front television room and put his brains on the curtains because he was all the time bitching about the paisley print anyway.

Joe stood quickly and said *what?* . . .

. . . And Danny told him to sit the hell back down. . . .

. . . So he did, but almost missed the top step. . . .

. . . And Danny told him what two men could do after explaining that Joe's wife had offered to pay thirty thousand dollars for the business. The woman had looked up Danny's uncle in the federal penitentiary where he was being forced to watch a black-and-white television for having forgotten to pay some taxes. She had gone there looking for somebody to end her husband's life, stupid life, she called it, thereby qualifying her for the big insurance payment. And Danny's uncle had passed the woman along to his nephew, who was having female trouble and could sure use the extra money.

As a matter of fact, the woman hiring Danny even looked a little like Dee Dee, particularly around the middles of the eyes, which were hard.

So what two males could do if they felt a kind of solidarity-type thing forming between them was work out an alternative arrangement whereby Joe could pay Danny more money and he'd go kill Carolyn instead.

How do you like *those* jalapeños?

Joe couldn't believe any of what he had heard and had to lean against a pillar on the front porch to keep from toppling over and into a flower bed. But he kept his poise well enough to tell Danny that he did feel a certain kinship-type feeling welling up.

But why more, he wondered, why couldn't he pay Danny the *same* as what Carolyn had offered?

Let me walk into *this,* Joe thought as he entered into negotiations with Danny; they'd see who walked out.

Danny said now hold on, and he said it with such a sinister tone that Joe actually did hold on—he held on to the porch pillar. Maleness was not the only thing Danny was feeling. He also had some feelings as a businessman who had given his word, even if it had been to a man-killer. So Joe had better not fuck with him concerning money.

Joe didn't.

Danny said he'd take ten thousand more and go kill Carolyn, and it would be very simple, just walk up to her and say hi and stick her.

Joe asked what if he couldn't afford the extra money?

Danny said he'd make Joe the same deal he had made Carolyn: He'd wait for the insurance, for the final payment, the insurance or whenever Joe got the money. Otherwise Joe, my man, you die.

Joe told Danny that he had himself a deal.

What else could I say? he wondered.

Nothing.

Some reconciliation. Some new life. Some surprise.

So when Danny asked where Carolyn was, he told him. Gave him a photo of his wife. Description of her car.

The Holiday Inn at the airport.

They stood and shook hands.

Danny said it was a good thing being men.

Joe said no, it was a *great* thing.

Danny walked off and Joe went inside and got the telephone, which had been ringing every few minutes all the while the two good men had been sitting on the front porch.

JOE ON THE TELEPHONE
At the desk in the television room

"Yeah, hello."

"Joe?"

"What?"

"Joe, is that you?"

"What? I can't hear. . . . ."

"*Run,* Joe. Get out of there right now, get out of that house this instant. . . . ."

"Carolyn? What's that noise?"

"It's a stinking airplane, Joe. This motel, this room, it's like in the infield at the airport, the lights in here actually shake and flicker. . . . ."

"There, that's a little better, Carolyn, I can hear you now. . . . ."

"Joe, get *out* of there. I've been calling every few minutes for half an hour. I was so damn worried. I'm glad you're all right. Joe, we haven't got time to talk. So you just listen. Run. *Please.* I mean it. Leave. There's somebody looking to shoot you. I did the same thing you did. I hired somebody to get you. Tonight. *Now.* God. And when I heard what you had done to me, I couldn't function there at the restaurant. . . . ."

"You just let me walk into this, Carolyn?"

"I don't know what I did, Joe. If I was pissed off and meant for this to happen. I'm off drugs for the first time in many months, Joe, so I'm not thinking too fast. All I know is thirty seconds after you walked out of the restaurant, I had to tell you, darling. I meant everything I said and did earlier. Now just get out of there. Run, Joe, come over here, I'm in room two-oh-two. . . . ."

"No, *you* run, Carolyn. . . . ."

"What? There's another airplane going over. Damn. All the engine noise. I feel like when I look out the window I should at least *be* somewhere, you know, somewhere different, as though I've been traveling. . . . ."

"Carolyn, listen to me. Get out of there. Leave that motel. *Fast.* . . . ."

"Yeah, Joe, that's exactly what I said, get out of there fast. . . . ."

"No, Carolyn. You don't understand. Can you hear me now?"

"Yeah."

"I turned him around. Get out of there in a hurry."

"What? What was that you just said? Turned him around? Turned who around?"

"The one you sent to shoot me and my new picture-in-a-picture television set with one bullet. Danny."

"You turned *Danny* around?"

"Sure did."

"*My* Danny?"

"Of course. It was that or try to dodge a few bullets on the front porch. Carolyn, for Christ's sake . . . . ."

"So now *two* people are coming to kill me?"

"Afraid so, baby. But he just this minute left. There's plenty of time. He was getting into a male-to-the-end mode. Your wanting me dead with such gleeful anticipation, it set off a guy thing in him, he must have thought there but for the grace of God goes my carcass. So for ten thousand more, he agreed to rethink the situation."

"You told him where I was? Where I *am?*"

"Carolyn, come on now, sweetheart. Think along with me a second. Because you said nothing at the restaurant. . . . ."

". . . . . Now a confused female with a substance problem, I can understand that kind of a person having somebody killed, but you doing it, that's a vicious bunch of bullshit, Joe. . . . ."

". . . . . Because you didn't *say anything*, Carolyn, I had the barrel of a gun pressed hard against the back of my skull."

". . . . . Stop him, Joe, don't let him come here and murder me, don't let him kill the one you love. . . . ."

"But I have no number for him. Do you?"

"No. . . . . Then stop *her.*"

"I don't know how."

"Somehow this doesn't seem fair, Joe, *two* people coming to kill me. You at the house, having cookies and milk."

"Cookies? What cookies?"

"Stop it, Joe."

"Carolyn, come on, baby, I love you more than ever, and it feels exactly like they're coming after me, too. . . . . "

"Joe, your sympathizing with me is really starting to piss me off."

"Darling, listen, the airport isn't *that* far from here so you'd better start getting your things together. . . . ."

"But damn, I just sat down."

"Now there is absolutely no reason to panic."

"They know what kind of car I drive?"

"They know . . . . . of your car, Carolyn, yes, I think so."

"Oh Jesus. . . . . So I have to steal a car to leave here, is that it?"

"I wouldn't think so. But I would hang up right now and get in your car and go . . . . . how about to that motel down by where our street goes under the expressway. I'll leave now. I'll be there waiting for you. . . . ."

"I don't know if that's good news or bad news, Joe."

Danny was nearing one of the worst moods of his pretty dangerous life.

On his happiest days, he could be extremely unpleasant. Tonight, this morning, whatever it was, he felt like taking all problems by the neck.

He was right here at this point in time: The woman he loved with every fiber of his being, Dee Dee, who was perfect in every way except for what she thought, had left, calling him a pitiful excuse for a human as she went out the door, threatening to sue him for promises not kept. Oh please. Why don't you think about something possible, Dee Dee. Next, he knew no halfway decent-looking women. All he knew were pigs, ugly damn things. Jesus, it looked like he was going to have to lower his standards. *Again.* Break up, lower standards, break up, lower, break up, lower, lower, *lower.* God in heaven, this time next year he'd be asking out a hunchback or a member of the Junior League.

And his new Range Rover costing almost seventy-thousand dollars sure *did* have a rattle under the dashboard, more like a click, actually, that you could hear every single time you put your foot over the clock and pushed forward.

There had been other recent car trouble as well.

It happened on the way here, at a stoplight.

Right, a good-looking woman was driving a cab. Danny ran the window down and waved to her and asked if she'd like to go out sometime. She gave him the finger and drove off, not something you'd see on a brochure in the new car showroom.

Left, somebody in the automobile there rolled down his window and said that was a pretty nice-looking vehicle Danny was driving, what was it, a new Isuzu?

Having his alleged engineering masterwork mistakened for some sweatshop tin was very insulting.

One more annoyance and the Range Rover was going back and into the showroom. Even if the dealership was closed at the time.

Finally, the possibility had begun to exist that he had been buddy-fucked, that he had made a mistake turning this business around and looking for the woman. Because she wasn't here, wasn't at the Holiday Inn at the airport.

Airport accommodations, God, there was a downer. The noise was a joke. When something took off or landed, floors vibrated. Trainee conventions, that was the only kind of business anybody in their right minds would do at airport accommodations. Hillbillies. People from hick towns might have high school reunions here. That was it.

And speaking of trainees, that was who ran the airport joints, kids just starting out in the food and lodging business, kids playing grown-up.

Danny asked the young man at the front desk if Carolyn was registered.

No sir, sir, there was nobody here by that name, Your Highness, thank you, come again, come back, good morning, good day, we love you, and if you want to fill out a card saying I was courteous, so be it.

This kid seemed to have come here directly from Front Desk School.

Danny then asked if any single women had checked in within the last couple of hours.

A look of grim concern came over the desk kid's face and he said sorry, sir, this information couldn't be given out.

Danny stared hard at him twenty seconds and then said *Boo*, scaring him badly, causing him to actually jump straight up several inches. The sight of somebody so genuinely frightened put Danny in a slightly better mood.

Then he drove around the motel looking for Carolyn's car, without finding it.

The motel was on open ground with no garages or neighborhoods or business areas near which or in which to hide a car.

It felt to Danny like the woman was not here.

Was gone.

So then he went back by Joe's house for what seemed like about the thirtieth time in the last few hours, finding nobody

there, either. He knocked on the front and back doors and got
some nearby dogs barking and left.

Finally he located somebody. This happened across the street
from the office building where Carolyn worked, in an alley.

He came upon a woman looking through some little binoculars.

DANNY AND TISH
Her rented car, across the street from Carolyn's office, a
quarter after three in the morning

"Don't even fucking move, woman."

"I won't. Talking isn't moving."

"Your head moved. It moved forward approximately five inches."

"It's the gun barrel you put on the base of my neck. It scared me."

"Oh really? Gun barrel? How do you know what a gun barrel feels like on the back of your neck, sight unseen?"

"I don't know what else would make you so tough."

"Hey, that's pretty funny. But I'm pretty tough naturally, for your information."

"Okay."

"Scoot over. All the way by the passenger door."

"I'm not doing anything wrong. . . . . "

"Oh really? After three in the morning? Sitting in an alley. Binoculars. What's over there, some kind of outdoor theater you're watching a performance of?"

"I'm a birder."

". . . . . You're a what?"

"Birder. Bird-watcher."

"Is that so."

"Sure. There was a Chilean meadow owl sitting on the southwest corner of that building. Two thousand, three hundred points. You get points for rare sightings. Helps you achieve a higher level of birding. You scared him away."

"Chilean meadow owl?"

"No doubt about it. Yellow tips on the wings. Burnt orange undercarriage."

"I'm afraid I'm going to have to call you on that."

"I'm sorry? I don't know what you mean."

"I think you're telling me a fucking whopper, there, partner."

"Why's that?"

"Turn the rearview mirror your way. You can see in the moonlight there. Your eyes are smiling. You held your face still pretty good during that Chilean bird bullshit. But you couldn't keep your eyes from twinkling."

"Yeah, I see what you mean. . . . . "

"That's it, that's the way, have yourself a nice big laugh."

". . . . . I'm sorry. . . . ."

"Here, use this Kleenex, it's brand-new."

"I don't know where that laugh came from. . . . ."

"You know, the birder thing had a chance. But your mistake was in not keeping it a little closer to home. I mean Chile, for Christ's sake. Owls fly what, three-quarters of a mile an hour? Time they got up here, they'd be too old to reproduce. Too old and too winded."

"People say the damnedest things with guns to their heads."

"Now listen here, woman. Don't get too relaxed and comfortable there. I just caught you lying. And I'm in the worst mood since my father killed my dog. But I do like your wig."

"Thank you. And I like yours more and in a better way."

Joe and Carolyn sat on the edge of their queen-size bed that had lumps and thought about what they should do next.

Do *now*.

Not next.

Because so far they had not done anything at all.

Except try to call off the people looking to kill one of them at the very least and, the way things had gone, probably both of them now.

They were not able to call either party, Danny or Tish.

Mind-boggling.

People trying to kill them.

People they themselves had hired.

People they could not call off.

They sat in room 22 at the Cheeseball Motel.

Or the El Siesta Motel.

Whichever.

Their room was square with a bed, a bedside table, a lamp, a desk, and a chair. A window unit half-heated the room. The window machine was off now. Carolyn had put it on High Heat and it sounded not much short of a jet engine, and she had had enough of that for the evening. The walls were cold brick, the floor tile. Old-fashioned lawn furniture was outside each room. Metal chairs. The desk had a Bible, a notepad, and a pencil in the top drawer. Something had been written on the notepad by a former roomer, for God's sake, and the message was still there. In big, bold block letters across the top of the pad was YOU'LL BE SO SORRY MOTHERFUCKER and on the bottom of the pad was HERE I COME READY OR NOT SO GET READY TO PERISH!!!!!

Upon finding these notes, Joe wondered if he should call somebody.

Carolyn said yes, call Orkins; since old notes were still around, she didn't want to touch anything, and she even spread all the towels from the bathroom across the bed before sitting on it.

If their emotional conditions improved markedly and they chose to have some sex here in the Low Rent Inn, they would most assuredly do it standing up, standing on the towels.

They were getting along fine.

Probably closer to all right.

Carolyn was still pretty pissed off about two people wanting to kill her and couldn't understand exactly how such a thing

had happened. Joe said that it was merely a technicality. They
were a family, they were as one. There was no way in the world
that he would even for a fraction of a second consider sneaking off and leaving her to deal with the two people wishing her
final harm.

Sneak fucking *off*, Carolyn said, what do you mean *sneak
fucking off?*

Like if they started arguing, Joe said; but since there was no
chance of it happening, there was no use in even mentioning it.

Mention it? Carolyn said. She hadn't *mentioned it.* She had
repeated it.

He told her to calm down and take his hand.

She got around to it.

Unable to call the killings off, they were fearful and sat close
together on the bed.

They thought about who knew what.

Both of those trying to kill them knew all there was to know
about work addresses and descriptions of cars and favorite
places.

They could be out there right now; could be, nothing, they
were out there.

And they could even be right outside the door. Driving down
the street. Walking around the block. And as if that wasn't depressing enough, and as if the stain on the bedspread wasn't
depressing enough, to top it all off was the sorry fact that they
didn't even know what in the hell the people trying to kill them
looked like. Either of them, Danny or Tish, could take off their
wigs and glasses and hats and change clothes and knock on the
door and say collecting for the Salvation Army without anybody thinking a thing.

Carolyn knew Danny's white Range Rover.

Joe knew Tish's white rented four-door.

Vaguely.

But he didn't even know its make and model.

They knew what their disguises looked like, basically, and
that was that.

After it became apparent that they weren't able to call any of this off, Joe went to the window and pushed the curtains aside, using a pencil because something sticky was there with a dead fly affixed to it, and he looked outside, reporting in an upbeat fashion in each instance that nobody was there.

Carolyn said we're so fucked, normal sounds like a report at which to rejoice.

Then she apologized, kissed her husband on his cheek.

Joe asked how she was doing without cocaine.

She said that besides the sensation that snakes were crawling around inside her head, she was doing all right.

She asked how he was doing without gambling.

He said no problem.

Carolyn made the point that once again it seemed like she was getting reamed in the reunion deal, giving up something that let her fly immediately off to a place where she was the judge and jury, while he gave up watching fat guys ram heads.

After all this took place, they sat quietly on the bed and listened to a television in the next room blare talk-show noise.

Joe said the worst thing he felt right now was an urgent sense of vulnerability.

He felt that they needed a purpose.

A focus.

They were getting along well enough and he sensed that if they could work together toward a specific common cause and bust the hell out of here, they were well on their way toward a useful life together; solve this, that's all he had to do.

So he created a goal for them.

It was his best idea ever, he said.

A lifesaver.

Carolyn was genuinely pleased to hear that; give your best-ever idea for fixing this to me now, she told him.

Joe's idea was that they go. That's right, he told her, they'd just up and leave like kids. Be spontaneous. Go *away*. To somewhere spectacular, to somewhere vibrant and scenic and temperate if possible.

They would *run away from home!*

Screw their debtors.

Here was what they would do. They would do what most adults fantasized about past the age of, what was it now, twenty-seven, twenty-eight—they would go to the bank, they would take out all that was there, they would buy a bag of new clothes each, and they would take off and soar to a new place and have some fun.

Carolyn listened to this and cocked her head one way and then the other, like a cocker spaniel who was enjoying the sound of something, but was having a little trouble grasping the specifics.

She very much liked the screwing-the-debtors part.

But what would they do for a living?

And, go *where?*

Joe said they'd do something simple for a living like outsmart tourists and retirees. Plant store. Sure. Buy a bush for two bucks and sell it for nine. How hard was that?

And as to where, God, that was the *easy* part.

The Carolina low country. Pat Conroy Country. Ocean rivers. Slow-motion sunsets. Marshlands protected by law from the blight of progress. Sand dunes. Sea turtles nearly as big as Volkswagen bugs. Palm-size shrimp. Sea breeze. Noisy surf. And heron making lazy circles in the sky.

Carolyn said thanks anyhow but she'd pass on this place where you had to step up to sea level because it was fast becoming known as a world capital for numerous things that she had no interest in, it was the Skin Cancer Capital of the World, for example, as long-time residents went about their business while cowering from the sun, while darting from shade patch to shade patch; and it was also the Arthritis Capital of the World, the next Florida, as old fuckers from the East and Midwest were packing themselves into the Carolina low country in record numbers. Whereas this area was indeed a nice place to dip into on holiday, the fact remained that at any moment in the summer, a hurricane could land and reduce all to toothpicks;

another fact to beware of was all the people Pat Conroy wrote about were deranged; and another fact was that one day all of the Carolina coastline would look like Hilton Head, an overdeveloped island mess of fast-food joints painted moss-colored in hopes of avoiding God's eye and escaping the wrath he holds special for the molesters of nature: a big old wall of cleansing water rising twenty-five feet overhead and moving forty miles an hour. No, on Hilton Head there were more Realtors than old guys taking nitro for bad hearts, if you could believe *that,* so Carolyn had to pass on spending the rest of her life in this portion of the world.

Well then, Joe said, Wyoming. Near-Sky Country. Where on a cloudless night you felt like you could stand on your toes and reach up and spin a star, the heavens seemed that close. Crawl on your hands and knees some morning deep onto a wild and woolly prairie like the one where they filmed *Shane,* and listen to the elk mate. It wasn't the specific sound that was worth the effort. Mating elk sounded something like the music played during the slashing scene in the motion picture *Psycho.* It was the sense of humor displayed by anybody crawling onto a cold dark prairie that made you feel good. More about Wyoming: Catch a trout out of a see-clear-through stream for brunch without having to count eyeballs and fins because of what some chemical company might have dumped upstream. Campfires. Cookouts. Horseback rides through the aspen. Eavesdropping on moose.

Yeah, well, what about the other ten months and two weeks of the year? Carolyn wondered. What about *winter,* which was all but the last week of June, the whole of July, and the first week of August? What about wind chills of minus *your nose?* What about all those alcoholic CEO spouses and their masks of artificial joy carved out by the plastic surgeons? What about all those four-wheel-drive vehicles that never got off the pavement except to have the oil changed at the garage? Carolyn said no thanks to Wyoming due to flying icicles. The last time they had been there on a winter wonderland weekend holiday, she had left her new tennis shoes outside the back door of their condo and they broke in half, froze right through. How in the hell could he have forgotten *that*.

Okay, Joe said. All right. Whatever. Fine. There was always Santa Fe. Howling coyotes on your coffee cups, plates, T-shirts, mirrors, stationery, underwear, hats, and license tags. Food with a sting. Cool nights. Art out the keister, the famous opera done out of doors in the moon rays. Let's see, there was something else. Oh yeah. Rattlesnake burgers.

God in heaven, Carolyn said, he had to be *kidding*. The only Indians not selling turquoise on the town square were the Cleveland Indians. And the western art, please, if she saw one more painting of a Great Spirit wafting up out of a peace pipe or a campfire, she'd take a damn paring knife to it. She'd have to be taken bound and gagged to this, the queen mother of America's tourist traps, where, after sundown, some of this land's Native Americans can usually be heard to say as they walked to their Suburbans after having wrapped their unsold turquoise and silver in blankets, "Can you believe those assholes from Cincinnati paid that much for those bracelets?"

All right, he heard her. Noted. Sedona then. Big red rocks. Like that.

Could she possibly have heard him correctly? Sedona was comprised mostly of an awkward mix of golfing grandmothers and pot-smoking hikers and New Age philosophy proponents who did nutty stuff like get up at three in the morning to go sit on one of the so-called forceful vortices located throughout the area, a forceful vortex being similar in appearance to plain old yards and lawns and mounds of dirt. But according to those hustling books and brochures full of earthy theories, and according to those running two-hundred-dollar jeep tours into the Sedona countryside, a vortex was made important by rock formations existing far underground. And if you sat right on one of the most forceful mothers, and your credit card had a good number and a buying balance, good intentions would run right on up to you and fill your heart and head and extremities with vibrancy. Or something like that. But Carolyn had already freaked out and had been a hippie. And she didn't want to go sit on a rock and look at people too young or too old or too stupid. Plus the desert was too damn dirty. Get Sedona the hell *out* of here.

Montana, then. Joe said everybody was talking up Montana in a real good vein. Lots of legroom. User-friendly fish. Slow quail. . . .

Carolyn said she wasn't going to take an airplane to the movie rental store, and that was all there was to it.

The Pennsylvania Dutch Country. It was like New England but without the prices and the letter sweaters and combination bookstore-cafés. . . .

Now just a minute, Carolyn said.

She didn't want to live on a tour bus route.

Because of early retirement and a high state of self-employment and a virtual explosion of old, rich people dying, and having their worthless children inherit the cash, too many Americans had too much free time on their feet and hands.

Yellowstone in February, that was about all that was left; the rest of the time it was bumper-to-bumper with suckers in recreational vehicles.

The pretty parts of this country were now and forever more officially screwed to sawdust with too much development and too many people.

For any privacy at all you had to give up comfort.

The only spots with much left were places like Oklahoma, where there were no tourists for a reason.

The new last frontiers had been created by abandonment.

Carolyn said she wasn't running off anywhere. She was going to stay right here.

DANNY AND TISH
Her rented car

"Now *what?*"

"It's the truth, Dan."

"Not Dan. Dan*ny.* And I don't believe you."

"Why would I lie?"

"I don't know. To keep from being robbed or killed. Those are both good reasons."

"Why would lying stop you from doing something terrible to me?"

"You could be trying to confuse me. Disarm me with misinformation."

"No."

"Well then, tell me again. All of it."

"All right. I'm from Kansas City."

"I've seen worse than Kansas City. Big enough to get lost in. But still small enough to maintain a sense of identity. You're a face in the group. Not a face in the crowd. That's my guess. Am I right?"

"No, that's pretty much bullshit, Danny."

"How can what I say be pretty much bullshit when I've got a gun?"

"It's a pretty typical big town, Kansas City. Not much down-home charm. It's probably closer in distance to a lot of country towns than are most other large cities. Maybe that's what you meant."

"You sound like my last girlfriend. Telling me what I meant."

"You're giving them up?"

"What?"

"Girlfriends."

"I don't think so."

"It was a joke. I'm very nervous. Sorry."

"No need to be sorry because I didn't get it."

"You said I reminded you of your last girlfriend. Like last as in final."

"So tell me what I meant."

"Your most recent girlfriend. Anyway. I'm here for the woman. Second floor, left, her office. Carolyn."

"This is a hard one to believe. You were hired by the husband?"

"That's right. Big gambling dummy. I beat him out of a nickel tonight myself on a basketball game."

"Me too."

"You too what?"

"I'm here to kill the woman also."

". . . . . . Oh, come on, Danny."

"Yeah. Actually it started out the other way around. She got me through my uncle, who's in a federal penitentiary for misplacing some of his tax information. The woman wanted the husband taken down."

"*Tonight?*"

"Yeah. But she started acting very anti-man and it got to me. My guess is she winds up fucking some dyke's breast."

"Interesting image."

"So instead of putting one through his ears, I turned it around for ten thousand more, a total of forty. But he never said anything about you to me. Was it Tish? That really your name?"

"Or Tisha."

"I guess the reason he didn't mention you was because I still could have shot him a couple or three times."

"Exactly, Danny, that's enough to keep anybody quiet. Had he mentioned me out here already, you'd have probably sent him along to the next world."

"Or to a maggot field of eternal nothingness."

"Or that, sure."

"So, Tish. What am I supposed to do now?"

"Marry me."

"We start splitting fees, half for you and half here, we go in together, we're down to migrant wages. You've probably got your down payment in your pocket there. For taking the woman out. So let me tell you about the percentage play from my perspective at this point in time. I shoot you dead, I take the money you've got, then I go find the woman and do that business as originally planned. Although the guy pisses me off some for not telling me about you out here. Not that I blame him actually, because as we both agree, had he told me, I could have run a bullet down his spine. Anyhow, you're the key to how this goes now. I guess I don't *have* to kill you. God knows there's no precedent to go by, no law of averages, not that I've heard. I could put you in the trunk and take your money and go complete the business with the woman. I know this is probably a tough question to focus on with my pistol touching the nipple of your left breast there. But what would you do if you were me?"

"..... I can't answer that, Danny. God *knows* I'm not going to say anything that might cause you to kill me. But on the other hand, I can't say that if I were you, I'd put me on the bus with an ice cream cone and the latest *People* magazine and pretend like none of this ever happened. If I were you? ..... I'd probably feed the turtles with me. So all I can do at this point is hope that you're a better person than I am, Danny, that there's more depth to your character, that you're more creative and have a more responsive heart."

"You ..... dating anybody, anything like that?"

"..... What?"

"You dating anybody? You with anybody?"

"No. No, I'm not."

"Married?"

"No."

"You're not one of those sexually erratic people, are you?"

"I'm sorry, what?"

"You're not a dyke."

"No. . . . ."

"I don't understand lesbianism. Not that any heterosexual man probably could too well. Believe it or not, I'm pretty old-fashioned when it comes to sex and things like that. My last girl-friend . . . . . my *ex*-girlfriend . . . . ."

". . . . . There you go."

". . . . . She got very pissed off when I explained my theories about lesbians to her."

"Which are?"

"Well actually, there's basically only one. The majority of your tried-and-true lesbians had pathetic fathers. Now I'm not talking about women you see licking on each other during various changes of life, you know, on the fuck films or at some concert where a famous female singer just came out of the closet by knocking a hole in the door with her ugly damn face. I mean, what do you expect with doggy-looking people. It's gayness or bust. Who can blame them. Now talking about the nice-looking ones, it's sexy watching two women do each other as long as they're open to the possibility of an actual male penis coming their way at some point in time. But two confirmed lesbians with absolutely no interest whatsoever in the one unique male attribute that cannot be simulated, which is the desire to fuck everything that moves, daily, and lie about it, forget it, watching serious dykes rub onto one another, this in my opinion would be like watching an autopsy."

"You seem to have given this a lot of thought, Danny."

"You're dating somebody who doesn't know the difference between homosexuality and bisexuality, what are you going to do."

"What is the difference?"

"Bisexuals are slightly better looking. Now where were we?"

"You were trying to decide whether or not you should shoot me and rob me, or fuck me."

"I was?"

"Maybe it's just wishful thinking, Danny."

"I bet that's what you tell all the guys rubbing your front with a gun barrel."

"It hasn't happened all that much."

"You're pretty nasty, Tish or Tisha, you know that?"

". . . . . I don't know how to answer."

"Can I tell you something personal?"

"Sure, I'm flattered. I hope."

"I'm attracted to you."

"Well Danny. Hell. I'm glad."

"Tell me this. What do you think about me?"

"Well. Now I know it might sound like I'm saying this simply to save my life. But I like you, Danny. A lot."

"Yeah?"

"So why don't you put that damn gun down or put it away and let's get to know each other a little better. Without prejudice."

"Oh, I don't think I could do that."

"Why?"

"Well, because at this juncture of our relationship, I trust me not to kill you slightly more than I trust you not to kill me, and then go take that woman down for all the money yourself. You said you liked me. What is it that appeals to you?"

"I'd have to say the first thing I like about you, Danny, is your straightforwardness. There's no hidden agenda. That's very reassuring. Very relaxing. You say what you think so nobody has to wonder where she stands. Also, I think your old-fashioned streak is absolutely charming in this day and age. . . . ."

"Jesus Christ, what do you think I'm doing here, interviewing for a job? What about the way I *look*?"

"I like your mouth. I like a full upper lip on a man. Take that

stupid damn wig off. . . . . Good *God,* you think you could
have gotten your hair cut a little shorter?"

"Burrs are fashionable, for your information."

"Who with, moms? Your chest looks fine. It's not all slick
like a woman's, is it? Good. I could have stood another inch on
you. What are you, five-ten?"

"Get out."

"Five-ten and a half?"

"I flew by five-ten and a half. I'm five-eleven, easy."

"Big, tough guy, huh. Can you back that up in the sex de-
partment?"

"You keep that attitude up and you'll never be able to meet
my mother."

"Really? That's too bad. Where's she live?"

"Heaven."

Let's see now, what were they going to do after they did it in
the car?

Oh yeah, that's right. Go to a beer bust.

God.

If Tish had done it in a car before, it hadn't amounted to
enough to remember.

Because she was going to do it in a car now, you bet she was,
because it had to beat being shot in the head; and just how much
doing it with this guy in the front seat of his fancy all-terrain
vehicle beat a slow and painful death was something she was
going to learn about right now.

Tish's rented car was cramped, and plastic, so she left it in the
alley.

Danny started to pull his Range Rover into a parking lot by
a city park, bless his goofy heart, probably to be a little bit ro-
mantic, as a big park fountain with waterfall sounds was close
by. But Tish told him that lots by city parks were festering
grounds for sexual perversions of all types and were regular
stops on cop patrols.

So then Danny took it to a metered parking space on a

through street that didn't have much traffic on it at this hour, which was after three in the morning.

Tish had never done it in a car parked at a meter on a through street, of that she was certain. And she had never done it with anybody pointing a loaded revolver at her, though a number of times she had felt such was the case, many times she had felt threatened into sex, but then who hadn't.

But a loaded pistol.

The heat was on on several levels.

Tish bet she wouldn't be critical of his technique, or fastness or slowness.

And man, the awkwardness of it all. People buying these expensive and fancy vehicles obviously had enough money to have sexual intercourse in some suite, not in the front seat.

This was the way Tish did it:

First, Danny put on a condom and had to use two hands to do it, and Tish thought about smacking him in the mouth and trying to wrest the gun from his right hand when it was busy gift-wrapping his business. But then she thought no, maybe I'd miss. And also, for a second or two tops, she thought about trying not to hit him on his teeth because, well, maybe he was good with his stuff there.

And she was immediately ashamed.

But that was what she felt.

Once he was sealed in tight, Tish sat on the console and put her right leg onto the dash over the speedometer and her left leg over the back of the driver's seat, not a ladylike position, but so what, this wasn't any first date. It was a last date.

Danny was able to come together with Tish by turning to his right and moving up under her, his left hand braced on the dash for lifting leverage, his other hand, gun included, squeezing her butt.

Definitely a new feeling, Tish thought, fingers squeezing a gun butt and your butt at the same time.

His presence inside her was not an entirely unpleasant experience the first few seconds, the uniqueness of the setting possibly having something to do with that, the shock value; then her mind raced ahead as did some of his.

She said you're not going to fuck me and then kill me, are you, and he said of course not; and then he said you're not fucking me just to stay alive, are you, and she said no way, she was genuinely attracted to numerous of his original characteristics, such as his carrying on a serious conversation while they were having sex; and then she watched intently as he reached that moment of male definition where the life force was passed from one to the next with the ejaculator experiencing a feeling that was unlike any other with the possible exception of taking the first bite of a hot fudge sundae as a horse you had bet your last cent on came home to win at odds of 75 to 1.

And everybody knew how often that happened.

About once every eighty years if you were lucky.

Male sex was so good because it seldom went *too* wrong, and when it came off correctly, it was a moment of perfection in an otherwise pretty amateurish world.

But one of its most pleasant asides got Danny in some trouble, and that was the closing of one's eyes at the onset of glory. It was almost like the penis and the eyelids were connected and when the former started producing, the latter closed. Maybe the closing of the eyes at the instant of ejaculation was part tradition so as not to embarrass either yourself or your partner at a very emotional time. Whatever. In the front seat of a fine vehicle costing almost seventy-thousand dollars that could run over dozens of golf balls or tennis balls at the club without sloshing out a drop of whatever you were drinking, rubbing around on some of the softest and sweetest-smelling leather ever, with Don MacLean singing "American Pie" on a world-class sound system, making it with a woman with tremendous legs, a pretty face and an ornery disposition, just *try* not to shut your eyes for a second or two in blissful ecstasy.

And when Danny gasped and moaned and thrust his hips upward and closed his eyes a couple of seconds as another of God's most used and appreciated gifts to man was gratefully accepted, Tish lunged forward at great personal risk, with her pretty legs still arranged at odd and almost opposite angles, and gave this guy her best shot with her closed fist.

She caught him pretty flush, her middle knuckle landing right on his mouth and causing something in there to move, and causing her hand to hurt. She really put her weight behind the right-cross punch and had a good deal of momentum, coming into the blow from her slightly elevated position atop the console, falling into the swing, her 122 pounds solidly behind it.

Knocked his silly ass sillier, that's basically what she did.

Danny of course was enjoying one of the best parts, if not *the* best aspect, of maleness, the giving of it to her; and when the shock of pain hit his face, the first thing he thought was that an object had probably fallen from a nearby building, a damn gargoyle or something, and had come through the windshield.

Since Danny was punched in the teeth during the supreme moment of sexual conquest and fulfillment, he was slow to react and Tish was able to get his right hand off her butt and bite it hard and grab the pistol and jump back to her side of the front seat and aim the gun right at his face and tell him that if he did anything else except quietly and slowly examine his injuries, she'd shoot him but good.

JOE AND CAROLYN
In their little room at the El Siesta Motel

"It's really pretty simple, Joe. We have to kill them."

"That doesn't sound simple to me."

"It's simple in theory. It's a simple solution."

"Carolyn, would you please quit looking out those curtains every minute or two. It makes me nervous."

"*Not* looking outside makes me nervous."

"So how about we compromise. Look out once every five minutes."

"All right, Joe."

"You really think trying to call it off would be virtually impossible?"

"Well Joe, for the love of God, we don't know *who* they are. *Where* they are. What they *look like*. We can't go up and down the street asking strangers not to kill us. . . . . What the hell are you doing, what are you looking like that for?"

"Like what? I'm not looking like anything."

"Yeah you are. You're looking kind of sheepish. Almost smug. When I said the word *us,* when I said we couldn't ask strangers not to kill *us,* you got a patronizing look on your face."

"I'm sorry then if I did. I apologize."

"You're not into survival like I am because you think I'm the only one they're after."

"Well Carolyn, if there's any degree of truth to that, it's inadvertent, it's subliminal."

"Let me help you get over that cocky attitude, Joe, so we can work closely together on this project. What I'm going to do now is take a piece of multistained stationery from this soiled desk and I'm going to write a quick note to the police saying that in the event of my untimely murder, you did it, you hired not one but *two* of them to get me. So in that case, Joe, I think I'd be better off dead than hanging with the lifers in prison. I saw a documentary on CNN the other night that said the latest rage was screwing new guy's ears in some of the male penal facilities, but there's probably nothing to it. . . . ."

". . . . You don't have to do anything like that, Carolyn."

"Well, Joe, humor me. What I'll do when we leave here is mail this to my friend Jill with an accompanying note that says if I get shot, open it. . . . . There we go, all done. Now. Let's go kill those cocksuckers before they kill *us.*"

"You don't think there's any way at all we could find them and try to get it called off?"

"No. But I suppose we could try to think of something. But my guess is the only way we could ever find them is as targets. Not as negotiators. When they come to get me. Us. So we have to be ready to kill them, not chat."

"Man . . . . ."

"We can't go through life wondering when and where they'll come for me, Joe."

"No. . . . ."

"We need to apply some closure to this motherfucker one way or the other; be done or be dead, Joe."

"Carolyn, could you just watch your language a touch there, sweetheart—you're swearing like a stand-up comic."

"Sure, honey. Talking dirty, I don't know, it seems to help me get in the mood for a shoot-out."

"I can't believe you'd actually write that letter. . . . ."

"Joe? Excuse the interruption."

"Yeah?"

"Scoot over here. That's a boy. Listen. I was just thinking in an offhand, half-assed way, like in an open-minded free-flowing stream of irrelevance that doesn't really mean anything. And in this new relationship of ours, I feel very comfortable sharing wild and random thoughts. So. I'm feeling a lot of stress, Joe, aren't you?"

"Sure."

"I mean, Christ, the start of our new lives together. People trying to kill us. Our trying to kill them. I have to be honest, Joe. I've never experienced pressure like this in my life. Not that it can't be used as a learning and caring experience that could solidify our love for one another for time immemorial. But you know those drugs I used to take?"

". . . . . Yeah."

"Those games and crap you used to bet?"

". . . . . Yeah."

"Well, Joe, sweetheart, listen to this. It just came to me while I was sitting here fearing for my life and, even more meaningfully, the life of my loved one. You, darling. What if we get ourselves some drugs and point spreads and fucking go nuts one last time, just blast ourselves right on up into a more fearless and confident level, hell, we could drink some beer and drug out and bet some basketball, Joe, just party ourselves into a state of arrogant bliss and then go out there and shoot those people's butts off, what do you think of *that?* . . . . .

. . . .
. . . .

"I mean, you know, it's just a thought. . . . .

. . . .
. . . .

"Just an idle thought . . . . .

. . . .
. . . .

"Okay. Fine. Screw it. All right?

. . . .

. . . .

"But you should have seen your eyes light up when I suggested betting some basketball."

"About killing them, Carolyn."

"Yeah, what about it?"

"It could be pretty hard."

"I know. We haven't even got a damn gun, Joe, not that the night clerk of this receptacle doesn't have a few for sale."

"I meant morally, too. I have a problem with the moral end of killing them. Us doing it. Personally. It's . . . . . frightening."

". . . . . Yeah, I know, Joe."

"I mean, it *is* us or them. We need to keep it on that level."

"Yep."

"But I don't know, Carolyn, it's just now that we're back together and have so much to look forward to, the moral aspect of it is worrisome. I want everything right for us."

"Well, Joe, come on now, it's not as though killing assholes is going to become habit forming like ice cream or cocaine. And don't forget that if we don't kill them, all we'll share is a grave."

"But if we do kill them, and there is a God, we could experience the torture of the eternal ovens of hell."

". . . . . That would hurt all right. Wait. I know what we need to do."

"What, Carolyn?"

"Find out if there is a God."

Tish handed the gun back to Danny and said that was the only way she was ever going to be able to make a point that he would believe: Smash him in the mouth and bite his hand.

Danny, frowning, bleeding, took the gun and pointed it back at Tish, who rolled her eyes, oh brother, it's one of the Flintstones.

Blood dripped from Danny's swollen upper lip onto his jeans and the leather seat of his sixty-six-thousand-dollar Range Rover. Blood also dripped from his hand onto the console.

Danny handed Tish the large front tooth she had punched right on out and into his mouth.

She tried not to grin but couldn't help it and said he looked like he had just gotten off a bus from Appalachia.

That pissed Danny off and his eyes filled with hard anger, replacing the damp humiliation that had been there as a result of having been socked at the exact moment of sexual release and satisfaction.

Tish told him to relax, an oral surgeon and a couple or three or four assistants and technicians could fix his tooth as good as new in, oh, eight or nine hours; she grinned again and said that in truth any old dentist could fix him in forty-five minutes to an hour, fit him for a fake like *that*.

He said it was easy for her to say relax, she didn't look like a cowardly hick.

He could not *believe* the disservice that she had done to womanhood as a whole with her abusive behavior; in the future when Danny was having sex, he'd probably duck and weave or even lean or jump back at the moment of sexual gratification.

Tish apologized for knocking out his tooth, saying she had aimed for the jaw in hopes of simply slugging him goofy, but had been thrown off line as she slid from the console. She said she'd pay to have his mouth fixed. And then she reminded him again of the most important thing she had done.

She had given him his gun back.

Now: Might he guess *why* she had given him his gun back?

His first guess was because she was stupid.

No.

Wrong.

Could it have been because she found him halfway interesting and maybe three-quarters of the way cute?

Yeah, as a matter of fact.

JOE AND CAROLYN
At an Episcopal church, in Father Bates's office, 5:00 A.M.

"Hello, Father."

"Hello."

"This is my wife, Carolyn. We really appreciate your time."

"You said on the telephone that you simply picked my name out of the telephone book. And that it was extremely urgent that we meet. Life and death, wasn't that the way you put it?"

"Yes. Before we start, I'd like to make a donation to your lovely church here."

"Thank you so much. There's always a lot in these old buildings in need of repair."

"I'd like to write you a check for one hundred dollars."

"Oh come on, Joe, give the man two hundred at least. It's like *dawn*."

"All right, fine, fine, two hundred it is. Here you go. I would have suggested such a sum myself. Except I hadn't blocked from my mind our dire financial situation."

"Thank you, Carolyn. And Joe. Now what can I help you with?"

"We need to know, urgently, if there is a God. And not one of those eye-of-the-beholder, yes Virginia, he's alive in the hearts of Christians everywhere, Santa Claus–type gods. Is there *the* God? Is there a real, tangible force who runs eternity?"

"Yes Joe, there is."

"You're sure."

"Yes."

"You're positive."

"Yes."

"Then why aren't I positive?"

"Faith is the foundation of God's being, Joe. Were God and His methods known as facts, then there would be no need for faith. The existence of a complicated but imperfect world is therefore proof of God's presence."

"We're not like big bugs."

"No."

"God made us."

"Yes."

"It would have been a lot simpler to say God made what we evolved from. Stepped in with Jesus to straighten a few things out."

"It's not so important what you think, Joe. It's important what you *believe.* Heart over mind."

"You're not saying that because it's your *job* to believe. That if you don't believe, you're out of work, you're putting handbills on windshields at shopping center parking lots?"

"No."

"If you didn't believe in God, would you fear dying?"

". . . . . Possibly. Probably."

"So then religion is your crutch?"

"No, it's my support. There's a difference. . . . ."

"Come on, Joe, we're not smoking joints in some coffee house. Get to it. What we need to know is what God is going to do, not if there is one. . . . ."

"I don't mean to be rude, and your donation was more than generous. But I do have a busy morning. . . . . "

"All right, all right. Here's the thing, Father. Some people are trying to kill us. . . . . Tell him, Carolyn."

"Some people we hired to kill each other . . . . ."

"But then we got back together and can't call it off. Isn't that right, Carolyn."

"Yeah."

"Now, Father, obviously if there's no God, we're fine. We can take the people down and get on with our lives. But if there is a God, and punishment, you know, whereas we think we're well within our rights to kill these people who are after us, as it's undoubtedly a self-defense posture, what we need to know is if God goes according to the law, or exactly how He looks at things like this. If it's self-defense under the law, are we absolved in God's eyes as well?"

"There is no killing in God's world, Joe. Wars are excepted. Certain professional matters like that. Survival matters."

"But there is forgiving in God's world?"

"Certainly."

"So here's the two-hundred-dollar question. Is there forgiveness even though a sin was made with a conscious effort?"

"Forgiveness must be asked for, Joe. And deserved. Earned, if you will."

"So we can ask for forgiveness *before* we kill the bastards who are after us and still qualify?"

"You can't *use* God, Joe."

"All right then, tell me this. What would you do if somebody came at you with a gun and you had the opportunity to defend yourself with a weapon? What if you knew in your heart that you could do much good spreading God's word, that you could give peace to the children, that perhaps as a great theorist and philosopher, you and God could save thousands of souls, but to do it you had to stop an evil person, to kill him. What, then, would you do?"

"Here's your two hundred dollars back, Joe. You've presented me with a problem too complex for me to comment upon with any degree of certainty."

Joe found her parked by a pay phone near a gas station that was closed.

He found her by asking himself, and Carolyn, what would I do, what would you do, if you or I were waiting for somebody to come home so I could nail one or more of them?

Carolyn said she would watch their house.

Joe said yes, but discreetly. You wouldn't hang near the house where you could be seen; you'd wait in reasonable proximity and make occasional passes by the dwelling in question.

So after Joe and Carolyn had driven by their house one way and then another, and after they had checked the side streets and side alleys, he went to the nearest through street that was four blocks away and he drove up and down that one.

And there she was. Sitting. Waiting. She was in a blue four-door this time, something that was similar in make and model to the white car she had been driving earlier.

Getting her was much harder than finding her.

They couldn't approach the woman sitting in the car so she could see them because she knew what they looked like and might just try to give them some bullets right there on the street.

Joe came up behind the car sitting parked near the pay phone in the gas station parking lot.

Carolyn let him out on the other side of the gas station, behind it, and then he crawled on his hands and knees from the corner of the building to the blue automobile. Since the driver's window was down, Joe guessed that the driver's door would be unlocked. It would help if it was. If he could yank open the door, he wouldn't have to reach in through the window and get the woman's neck, Tish's neck.

The driver's door *was* unlocked.

Joe crawled up to it from the rear of the car. Took a deep

breath by the back bumper, then crept onward. Put his left hand on the driver's-door handle. Pulled hard and fast. Swung open the door. The woman was leaning on the door with her left elbow and almost fell out. He was on her in an instant and got her in a choke hold and dragged her out of the vehicle.

Joe told Tish he was real sorry their relationship had to end this way, but you see, he was back with his wife and didn't want her killed. Plus he wanted his money back, the deposit. They had some outstanding debts that required their immediate attention. Now, if she would go away, if she could convince them that the arrangement could be called off and that they would never be bothered again, just possibly something could be worked out concerning Tish's living some more.

But at this point, it looked like a long shot.

If she wouldn't refund the money, and there was no pleasant way to put this, they were going to have to do to her what he had originally hired her to do—they were going to take her down, and then go do the same to Danny boy.

Pretty strange, huh; but such were the twists and turns of married life, very unpredictable.

Carolyn had been watching from a secure vantage point behind the gas station and raced forward in their car once she saw that Joe had Tish in a secure headlock.

Joe quickly rolled her into the backseat and Carolyn gassed it and got them out of there fast, got them home, where they took Tish inside and put her in a chair in the middle of the kitchen and listened intently as she told them that she was not Tish.

JOE, CAROLYN, AND THE WOMAN FROM THE CAR
The kitchen, 7:00 A.M.

"Did you see Danny?"

"Who is Danny?"

"Did he find you at Carolyn's office?"

"Who's Carolyn? What's her office?"

"Danny is the man my wife here paid to kill me. But he didn't like her."

"I don't know what you're talking about. And I'd like to ask you to please quit frightening me any more than you already have."

"Danny agreed to turn it around for more money."

"Turn *what* around?"

"The bullet. The job. The murder."

"Listen, friend. My name is *not* Tish. My name is Sheila. You've made a mistake. Now please. Don't talk anymore about what you people are doing to each other or to somebody else. When all this shakes out, I don't want to have any information that the police will want to hear."

"Shoot her, Joe, then let's go drag Danny's dumb ass out of whatever bushes he's in and do the same thing to him. Then let's go on a second honeymoon."

"Where to, baby?"

"Oh, somewhere remote. Finland, how's that sound?"

"Just odd enough to be fun. . . . ."

"*Listen.* Please! I am *not* who you think I am."

"You have no identification."

"No . . . . . it's home. I just came over here on an impulse. I told you. I don't trust my boyfriend. I went by his house to see if anybody was with him. . . . . "

"Where's your wig?"

"What wig?"

"Where's the hat? Glasses? The other clothes? The other car? Where's my money?"

"I've never seen you before in my *life.*"

"You took me to the basketball game."

"I did *not,* you lunatic."

"Joe, excuse me, can I speak to you a moment over here. . . . ."

"I want my money back."

"I don't have it. I never had it."

"You'll regret you said that. Stay there. Don't move. . . . ."

"I have to be at work in an *hour and a half.* . . . ."

"Joe . . . . . "

"Keep your voice down, Carolyn."

"Joe, let's step in the hallway. . . . ."

"All right, that's better."

"Are you positive it's her? She seems pretty, I don't know, sure of who she is."

"Carolyn, that woman is going to be very good at lying, at play-acting."

"You said she was covered up."

"But the cheekbones are the same. The eyes. Now, the voice does sound a little different; it's higher. But she's doing that to try to save her life. She's acting. It's her."

"Now, you realize that at this point in our life that we don't need to be kidnapping the wrong person off the street, Joe."

"It's her, Carolyn. . . . ."

". . . . . Listen there, mister, stop looking at me like that, you *crazy man.* . . . ."

"I just want you to be sure, Joe."

"I am. No doubt."

"Okay, fine."

"Now listen to me, Tish....."

"Stay away from me. I am not Tish. My name is Sheila Kizer. I work at a bank. My boyfriend is a prick. What else do you need to know?....."

"We want it called off, Tish."

"You want *what* called off, you....."

"No more name-calling or I'll thump you on the head with the butt of this gun."

"You want *what* called off.....*sir?*"

"The murder of my wife."

"Then you've got it."

"I mean it."

"It's off. Over. Done. I can't imagine what I was thinking in the first place."

"And I want the deposit back."

"And you shall have it. Now, how much was it?"

"Six thousand dollars. You know that. You took it."

"Sure."

"Where is it?"

"Home. It's home."

"Home? Which home? You mean your home in Kansas City?"

"No. Motel."

"What motel?"

"Hilton."

"Joe, lean over here."

"What?"

"She's lying. She's not going to call this off. Give me the gun. I'll shoot her right here and fucking now. I'm not walking around scared the rest of my life."

"Easy, Carolyn."

"No, bullshit, give me that gun and go sit down....."

"Carolyn, wait, I believe her about calling it off."

"Not me. I don't. Look at her eyes shifting around like that. She's not calling anything off. She simply wants out of here and is saying anything to get there. Just make yourself useful. Go get some wet rags and get ready to clean up the mess she's going to make. . . . ."

"*Don't kill me, please.* . . . ."

"Carolyn, don't shoot her in our home. . . . ."

"Oh, quit being such a pussy about this. Turn your head if you have to. . . . ."

"Wait a second Carolyn, the phone's ringing. I'm going to answer it. Don't shoot her while I'm on the line."

"All right, get it, Joe. Make it fast. I'm psyched up to get this over and done with right now."

"Okay, keep it quiet. . . . . Hello. . . . ."

"I have four cats at home. If you shoot me . . . . ."

"I can't stand cats, now be quiet. . . . . Who is it, Joe?"

". . . . . It's Tish. . . . ."

Sheila Kizer said that she would take five thousand in cash and forget that two people had dragged her out of her automobile and had then pressed the delivering end of a pistol to her head and had threatened to blast the life from her on numerous occasions.

It was that or call the police on them and have them taken away and put away, in which case she would only receive satisfaction, which would pay no bills; and then, too, she would have to explain to her boyfriend Chuck that she had been spying on him at dawn on the morning in question.

So Sheila went the five grand route, and got, in addition to a profound apology, the invitation to drop by for dinner anytime, plus the check.

Stopping at the front door as she left, Sheila said there was one more thing. She wanted Carolyn's sweatshirt, a nice muted-brown Donna Karan number. So Carolyn took the sweatshirt off her person and tossed it to Sheila, who looked around the front room at some lamps.

Joe said that would be sufficient and closed the front door.
Once Sheila Kizer was gone, all four of them got on the tele-
phone at once, there being two extensions at each place,
Danny's condo and Joe and Carolyn's house.

Joe spoke first.

He spoke calmly, asking how Danny and Tish had met, had
gotten together.

Danny, speaking as calmly, told him—he had gone by Carolyn's office and had found Tish waiting there, armed and
pissed. They had, um . . . . . introduced themselves, as any two
meeting in an alley at three or four in the morning might. Had
found out that they were after the same thing. Things. Carolyn.
And money. And so what the hell, who could have said, here
they were. Rather . . . together. Kind of . . . you know . . . *dating*.

Joe said good God.

Danny laughed and said yeah, no kidding, that was an un-
derstatement.

So did Tish.

Okay, Joe said next. He was going to take it from the top.
He said that he really appreciated their efforts, Danny's and
Tish's. They had obviously worked very diligently on their respective assignments. But certain things had changed. Joe and
his wife were back together and were working hard to rid themselves of their previous personal flaws and build a solid relationship steeped in trust and high ideals that could carry them
all the way to their decrepit years. And now that their partner's
happiness was a priority, it was obvious that they didn't want
each other harmed or anything close to killed.

So they wanted it called off.

They wanted it all called off.

Now.

Joe didn't want his wife harmed. She didn't want him
harmed. Period. End of paragraph. Amen.

Carolyn said to Danny, oh by the way, he was one of the

biggest twerps she had ever seen, his word as a businessperson not counting for crap.

Danny said it was a good thing he *was* a man's man and just a touch greedy or Joe would be dead now and she'd be famously rich with insurance money and none of this would be happening: Mr. and Mrs. Ozzie Nelson wouldn't be reunited.

Joe got the conversation back to where it needed to be.

Off, they wanted it called off.

Off? Danny said.

Off? Tish said.

Joe said correct. And of course Danny and Tish would be paid expenses and a reasonable stipend.

The line went quiet quite a few seconds, then a few more.

Then Danny cleared his throat and said well, here was what he thought about that. And he encouraged his associate to break in with a contribution anytime she felt the need.

Off?

Expenses?

Stipend?

No.

Now, off—perhaps.

Expenses—of course.

But reasonable stipend, fuck you people.

A *reasonable stipend* was what you gave somebody who didn't know any better, a simpleminded heir of a recently deceased billionaire, perhaps.

Danny said that there was one way in which they'd call it off and that would be for money, a lot of money, more, even, than what it would have cost to have the both of them killed originally and individually.

It would cost one hundred and fifty thousand dollars to call it off.

Joe yelled: A hundred and fifty thousand dollars for *nothing?*

Danny said no, not for nothing. One hundred and fifty thousand for the gift of *life.* Which was suddenly more precious now that each of them had the other to live for—the gift of *two* lives.

Tish laughed.

To reiterate, Danny said it was going to have to to go either one of these couple of ways:

One, Danny and Tish would be paid one hundred and fifty thousand dollars to call it off, or:

Two, they'd kill one of them for nothing, either Joe or Carolyn, vote on it maybe, flip a coin, who knew; and then they'd turn the other one over to the cops because they had it all on tape, the negotiations for the killings—whom did they think they were dealing with here, beginners?

The news that a tape or tapes existed of their hiring of murderers took Joe and Carolyn by terrible surprise and they didn't know what to do and didn't want to say anything that could be construed by the others as signs of weakness or dumbness, so they said nothing for fifteen seconds, the silence itself turning out to sound pretty dumb and weak.

Then Joe thought out loud, saying they didn't have the one-fifty. They owed bookmakers and drug dealers and were thinking about vacationing to Finland; a hundred and fifty thousand, *please*.

Danny said he was no financial counselor, but if he were either of them and possibly facing arrest for attempted murder, he'd be on the telephone to banks and other financial institutions, talking about such tools as second mortgages, or talking to wealthy relatives about loans.

Rather than think out loud anymore and further weaken their position, Joe said they'd get back to them, and Danny said no, *we'll* get back to *you*. They had the upcoming full day to get the money. Danny said he'd call at this time tomorrow to discuss the specifics of the transfer of the required funds.

As they hung up, Joe and Carolyn heard Tish say to Danny in a suggestive manner, you did good, now come here to me, baby.

It would have been a surprise if Danny *hadn't* fallen for Tish because he hadn't met many attractive women he didn't want

to marry and try to shape into his idea of a perfect wife. Males
in Danny's family had been becoming alcoholics and trying to
shape women into ideal spouses for as long as he could remember; it was like a tradition. But thanks primarily, in
Danny's humble opinion, to homosexual television talk-show
hosts and lesbian counselors, women no longer viewed being
a good mate as a priority. The contemporary woman had
blurred the line distinguishing males and females, and so now
this was becoming a genderless society based on intense personal and professional competition, the number one cause of
burnout and divorce.

But this Tish, she was different.

She wasn't looking for any man to blame.

She was like a female Danny, herself, and the most sexually
aggressive woman he had ever had the great pleasure to watch
walk around naked, which she said she liked doing, not because
of any pseudo-naturalistic bullshit, but rather because it made
her feel wicked.

She guessed that she was attracted to Danny because he was
so consistently worthless and probably couldn't sink much
lower than where he began the average day, and therefore break
her heart. Plus she kind of actually liked guys who thought they
were tough.

After the telephone call, they were both feeling very good
about their chances of making some pretty good money with
a minimum of effort, so Tish took off her clothes and went to
the kitchen and made them a couple of omelets.

The one thing they had to concern themselves with was the
possibility that Joe and Carolyn might opt to try to kill them
instead of paying the money.

Danny said they couldn't have that.

After breakfast, Tish wanted to go out onto the balcony of
Danny's condo and have sex with him standing behind her sixteen floors up as she stood at the rail wearing his robe, just like
they were admiring the view. Danny wondered if she was too

sexually advanced for him and she said probably. Now be quiet and start catching up.

So that's what they did.

While they were having sex and searching the clear early morning sky for shooting stars, Carolyn sat on the sofa with her face buried in her hands, wondering if she had ruined her life by going off drugs and not having her husband killed.

And Joe called the police.

JOE AND DETECTIVE WATKINS
Joe on his telephone in the kitchen, Detective Watkins on his
phone at his desk at work

"This is Midtown. Detective Samuel Watkins. Help you?"

"Yeah, listen, I've got a couple of questions."

"Is it an emergency?"

"Uh, well . . . . ."

"That tells me it's not."

"It could be an emergency very soon. And it is from a psychological perspective right now."

"Hang on a second and let me get rid of this other call. . . . . All right, what's your name?"

"Joe. . . . ."

"Joe, honey, excuse me, Jesus Christ. . . . ."

"Just a second, Detective . . . . . I'm sorry, who?"

"Watkins."

"Detective Watkins, yes, excuse me a minute. . . . . All right, Carolyn, what is it?"

"Joe, I've got a great idea. Why don't we not tell the police our names. Doesn't that sound like fun?"

"It was just my first name."

"Just don't let anybody talk you out of anything valuable."

"Fine. . . . . Detective Watkins?"

"Yes."

"I'm back."

"What is it that you need? I don't mean to be rude, but we're really busy this morning. It's like some of the bastards know exactly when the shift ends and start a lot of trouble during the changeover."

"First of all I'd like to know if this call is in any way being monitored, taped, or anything like that?"

"No it isn't. Should it be?"

"No. Now, you're not using one of those phones where it records the number calling in, are you?"

"No. This is just a simple in-and-out telephone on my desk."

"Okay. Good. Now here's what I called you about. Let's assume somebody hired somebody to kill somebody else. . . . . "

"Joe, excuse me. Is this a hypothetical situation we're talking about here?"

"What does it matter? The answers to my questions will be the same if the situation is real or the subject of a school paper."

"You sound, I don't know, a little experienced for school."

"Let's say I'm doing a master's thesis."

"It matters whether it's real or not because the hiring of a murderer is a crime, a very serious and tragic and cowardly crime. If somebody's life was at stake, my answers would be very much different than if it were a casual and theoretical question."

"Nobody's life is at risk."

"All right. Good."

"Too much."

"Now, Joe . . . . . "

"What I need to know is how the law would regard it if a person hired somebody to kill another person and then called it off."

"Hiring somebody to kill is against the law."

"But nothing ever came of it."

"Did money change hands?"

"Money? Yeah. It did. In the hypothetical situation."

"Did you get your money back? And let me just bring it to the present and personal tense for convenience."

"All right. And no, the money wasn't returned. Yet."

"Somebody hired somebody to kill somebody else. Money was paid for the work. The person doing the hiring and wishing the killing done then decided to call it off. But no money was returned. That about it?"

"Yeah. About."

"Hold on. . . . ."

. . . .

"He put me on hold. I guess he's checking the legal end of it."

"Hearing this discussed aloud, it takes on a whole new perspective. It's a wonder we haven't broken completely down."

"We're probably too tired. Seems like a pretty nice guy, this cop."

"They're nice about anything that can go in their memoirs. Their books, it's their only reason for living."

. . . .

"Joe? Detective Watkins. I'm back."

"Yeah, I'm here."

"It's a crime, Joe. Refund or no refund."

"You're sure."

"Yes. Look at it this way. Say you hired somebody to kill a person for you. You changed your mind. They didn't believe you. Shot and missed. That doesn't let you off the hook. Once the deal has been done, it's attempted murder. It can't be assumed that a contract is off. It's a very serious felony, plain and simple."

"Well hell, okay, thanks."

An important part of the rehabilitation of their marriage was to be a daily one-hour session where they sat down together and were thoughtful of the way each other was feeling.

So that's what they did now; after sleeping a few hours, they pulled back a couple of chairs at the kitchen table and Joe made a large bowl of fresh fruit—blueberries, blackberries, pineapple, kiwi, cantaloupe, raspberries, and honeydew melon—putting all of that and two plates and two spoons and a big pot of fresh coffee between them.

The premise here was that if you made the time to be thoughtful and considerate and attentive, then after a bit it would become second nature. And fun.

Carolyn spoke first at the beginning of their daily family meetings, and this was what was on her mind:

There was an extremely high degree of probability, like around 98 percent Carolyn guessed, that Danny and Tish would continue to extort money from them beyond the original demand. If it was indeed true that they had taped evidence of a crime being committed, of a murderer being hired. And, being deceitful and conniving, why wouldn't they have such a tape? And why wouldn't they use the tape or tapes, and the threat of them, each and every time they needed twenty grand, thirty?

There was no reason why they wouldn't do that, and so they had to be killed.

Next on Carolyn's concerned mind was this relationship, this extended marriage, this whatever it was, and right now it seemed like a clunker that had been taped together and was running on fumes.

Specifically and bluntly, Carolyn was concerned that they had made a big mistake getting back together and trying to make a partnership out of what had been a border war.

A truce was about all she could ever see for them, not a damn foot massage.

She was afraid that she would have been much happier by herself or with a new man in her arms, with a new life, a new career. She was worried that they would fall back into their old habits and patterns because once you had crossed a line, once somebody had been seriously wounded, once something you held dear had been damaged, there's no recovery, only revenge.

Oh sure, being truthful and honest and open, it *sounded* like they were a new couple. Sometimes. But what if he was nuts, what if it was a con, what if he got her back and started missing being an asshole? How did you change memories?

So there.

She was very depressed because she might have to go kill two people and then divorce her husband and be at a job she hated.

So relate.

Get considerate.

Be thoughtful.

She dared him.

And this was what he thought:

It would have been much better if they had started their new lives together with something like a Caesar salad and a well-written movie featuring original characters, great scenery, and a surprise ending, and not this, not a struggle to live, which, he agreed, now involved the elimination of two very dangerous bottom feeders on what amounted to their home court.

What was different, however, was this, the very act of sharing, so one person wouldn't have to guess how the other was feeling and thinking, and come to panicky conclusions based on insecurities.

For the first time in many months, Joe knew how Carolyn felt.

And unfortunately it really pissed him off.

Couldn't she *possibly* do something besides just *complain?*

At this point in their first sharing experience, where Joe was explaining to Carolyn how he felt about her sourpuss, self-serving, and almost mentally unbalanced attempts to infect their relationship with her problems, her fears of death, old age, and professional boredom, Carolyn told him to take their first caring meeting and shove it up his butt.

So then they sat quietly and ate the fruit and drank the coffee for about a quarter of an hour before declaring the meeting about restoring the finer qualities of humanity to their relationship off limits to personal matters and the feelings they attracted.

After that, talking from their heads and not their hearts, matters went pretty well.

They decided that the first thing they would need in order

to kill the two people out to ruin their lives was a gun with no serial number. They weren't going to choke them. They had a gun at home that was registered to both of them. They needed something that could not be traced.

So that became number one on their list of Things To Do Today that Carolyn put on the appropriate page in her daily planner.

1. Get gun (that cannot be traced).

The day before yesterday, Carolyn's list of things needing to be done was this:

1. Grocery store.
2. Pick up dry cleaning.
3. Don't buy a cat.
4. Call house roofers for estimates.
5. Repel depression.
6. Change oil in car.
7. Get vacuum bags.
8. Ignore clicking sounds made by central air/heat unit.
9. Dentist appointment.
10. Extension cord.

Today's list was filled out this way:

1. Get gun (that cannot be traced).
2. Check bank for quick second-mortgage money for killers/extortionists.
3. Get bullets.
4. Formulate plan for killing those wishing to ruin us.
5. Get all credit cards with cash capabilities and run them right to the limit.

6. Purchase a couple of bullet-proof vests at army surplus.
7. Pray.
8. Silencer for gun?
9. Steal car license tag.
10. Water plants.

Joe said that he would get the gun and bullets and silencer and called his bookmaker, Cooper, for help with all of it.

As the *gentlemen's* clubs of the Eastern Seaboard had been replaced by the private jets, and as the brow-and-jaw boys were retired or dead—the ones whose brains through inactivity had turned partially to stone, forcing foreheads and chins to grow inordinately so that when seen from the right, their profiles looked like big C's—as the Las Vegas and big-city rascals went out of style and were replaced by people better with their cursors than their dukes, so too had the trend toward gangster sophistication trickled down to the bookmaking industry.

Tugboats with Nellie Fox–model Louisville Sluggers, baseball bats with thick handles so they wouldn't break when hit hard on a head, were no longer key players in the illegal gambling business.

Guys like Cooper were running things, thirty-year-old men with wives and children, math men, people who preyed on a few of the most accessible human frailties, the desire to make some easy money, and the inabilities to keep going when you were ahead or quit when you were behind. Only people without emotion, invaders from space, could consistently win money gambling, which explained why bookmakers did so well; emotion, a plus everywhere but gambling.

Cooper had a wife with StairMaster calves and kids in a private school, and on the street he could have easily been mistaken for law-abiding.

But he was a big-time bookmaker and therefore dangerous by nature, by tradition, if not appearance.

Disputes over money owed between customers and the bookmaker could fast turn into kid stuff: I'm not paying. Yes you are. No I'm not. Are. Aren't. Well, if you don't, you can't bet anymore and I'll have your wages garnished. Yeah, well, you do and I'll call the cops and turn you in. So that, the possibility of a wipeout coming so easily, the fact that a lucrative living could be lost by a tattletale, was why even in a day and age of electronic crime and crooks with Ph.D.s and Range Rovers, the fact still existed that if you didn't pay, something had to happen. With Cooper, first you got understanding. Compassion. You a little short? Take your time. Let's come up with a plan whereby you can sell some family treasures and heirlooms. The longer a debt went unpaid, the quieter Cooper became, the more philosophical; and the closer the implied threat of retribution seemed to move toward the surface.

In fact, the more articulate and physically unimposing the bookmaker, the more dangerous his potential, at least that was the way it seemed to Joe with Cooper.

When Joe asked about a gun, Cooper was friendly as always, asking if their business was about to be settled, that business being Joe's paying of the eighteen thousand. It had been Cooper who had set Joe up with Tish, and so obviously he was very interested in any news as to how that project was going.

Joe, trying not to sound like he was lying all that much, said it was proceeding all right and should reach its rightful end soon, with the money owned Cooper being available in good order. In the meanwhile, Joe needed help with a gun, an orphaned weapon, one with no traceable history.

And again, it was the nature of Cooper's response that made Joe feel as though a goose had not only stepped on his grave, but had also scratched around on it before taking a leak on his headstone.

Cooper said no problem with the gun; he'd have one ready in an hour and would have it sent over to the house and would simply add the cost to Joe's balance due.

Joe hung up and breathed shallowly and saw not only his life pass before his mind's eye, but also the lives of those on his block, everybody within exploding distance.

Carolyn's uncle was an official at the bank where they had their house mortgage, and she went there and said that she wanted as much second-mortgage money as she could get, as soon as possible, and if there was any delay, she would tell her aunt who her uncle was fucking on the side, the ignorant one with the good legs. She didn't know that he was fucking anybody, but he was an egomaniac without cause, which usually spelled a-i-r-h-e-a-d, and so she went with the law of averages. Flushed and floundering, he said he'd get back to her. Confident and cocksure, she said he'd better get back to her, and not with an excuse; with the second mortgage money in cash.

She apologized for threatening to ruin the tidbit of remaining fun in the man's squirrely little life, but she was in a life-threatening situation here. And then she kissed him on the cheek and left, thinking that what somebody could do at some point in time was simply get a telephone directory and turn to as insecure and irrational a group of professionals as you could ever hope to find, some people who didn't come close to deserving the money they were making. And who might that be? Dentists, sure. You'd look up dentists in the Yellow Pages and call one after the other, cold and randomly, and say that for ten thousand dollars you can have the evidence I have of you fucking around on a loved one.

And what was the national average of marriage or relationship cheats this year, half? So half of the dentists would probably bring the money. And the evidence of their infidelity, the proof, would be in their actual presence.

Snap a Polaroid of them sitting there with the payoff, there's your proof, nice doing business with you.

Walking from the bank, Carolyn wondered if perhaps she had a future in thinking up weird stuff.

They of course didn't want to give any money at all to the other two calling for it, to Danny and Tish. They wanted to kill them instead, shoot them, right off. They were prepared for that from a moral standpoint. But in the event that they had to show the cash, or turn it over as they followed along behind, they couldn't fool around with chopped-up newspapers, not with their freedom at stake. They had to have a bag of easy money ready, as instructed.

Both were certain that after further review, God would study the angles and forgive them 100 percent.

The remainder of the afternoon they went over their plan, which was to shoot the others in the fastest and easiest and safest manner possible, *bang*, right in the mouth.

And while Joe and Carolyn were getting their shooting faces on, Danny and Tish were at his place, and she was walking around naked as the man of the condo gave his full attention to trying to keep Joe and Carolyn from trying to kill them, a dead certainty; rather, a live one.

Danny found it hard to focus on work with Tish performing routine duties such as watching television and making sandwiches while so wholeheartedly naked. But Tish told him that concentrating on two things would make him sharper with each.

And Tish continued to become more enamored and charmed and comfortable with this character's open baseness and lock-jawed stubbornness and a lifestyle where no surprises seemed so appealing, where the only hidden agenda could be a distant move toward niceness.

CAROLYN AND JOE, DANNY AND TISH,
JOE AND DANNY ON THE TELEPHONE
Joe and Carolyn's house, Danny's condo, noon the following
day

"Hello?"

"Joe?"

"Yeah."

"Danny here. You sound a little down, man, you all right?"

"I'm fine. Not that it's any of your concern."

"Joe, come on now, the only reason not to be kind is if one of us is looking to upset the other one. So tell me this. How are you and the wife doing with the big reconciliation? You're in my heart and thoughts, man, I've got to tell you that. You building a strong foundation of truth and sharing on which to construct a future of honesty and openness? That about it? Crap like that going on pretty much around the clock?"

"We . . . . . fine. . . . ."

"Not us, man. All we're sharing is, I don't know, tongues. I guess we're going about it a little backwards, you know what I'm saying? All we're basically doing is sex, Joe. I mean it. I've never heard or seen anything like this woman, she's the strongest thing I've ever come across on a screen or a page, she's just sincerely wicked. I think part of the reason she likes me is because I'm such a horrendous individual in certain circumstances, such as my closed-mindedness about people of the same penis persuasion, you know, withs and withouts pairing off with each other. In fact she's said it, Joe, she's said I'm so goofy and screwed up about some things that the *slightest* bit of education would be a big improvement. Let her think what she wants, right? I mean, God Almighty, Joe, let's just *see* if I'm going to get tired of seeing her naked. Let's check it out. Let's test it. But hey, man, I'm rambling. It'll just be interesting to see which turns out the best way, won't it, you people doing it with your discussions and interactions and us over here basing a relationship on nothing but screwing and staring."

"Hang on one second."

"What's wrong, Joe?"

"I want to tell Carolyn something."

"Sure, no problem."

. . . .
. . . .

"Carolyn?"

"Yeah."

"They're over there having sex nonstop."

". . . . . You're kidding."

"No. He sounds like he's sixteen years old."

"Good. If they're all loved up, then maybe I can shoot them both with the same bullet. . . . . ."

. . . .
. . . .

"Danny?"

"Right here, Joe."

"I'm back."

"All right. Let's go to work."

"Wait a second. There's something I want to talk to you about. You need to think about this, Danny, it gets back to the male thing we experienced on my front porch. It's a feeling one man gets for another, a fellowship, an inherent brotherhood kind of thing, a fear for your well-being. I connected to you, Danny. And I'm worried, my friend, that she's after the money."

"Money? What money?"

"This money. The money you want from us, Danny."

"She's *after* it?"

"Yeah, Danny, Christ. Come on, think like a man."

"You mean, she might want the money, like, all for *herself*?"

"Yeah, it's a male instinct. . . . . . "

"Stay there. . . . . "

. . . .

. . . .

"Tish?"

"Yeah, babe, what is it?"

"Where are you?"

"Kitchen."

"I've got Joe on the phone."

"Great. You tell him what to do with the money?"

"Not yet. Tish, listen, he says you're having sex with me for the money. Said it was a male thing he felt. You going to try to take the money from me, Tish, is that the deal, is that why you're performing routine household functions in the raw?"

"No, sweetheart. I'm having sex with you because it's fun."

"Well . . . . ."

"He's only jealous; there's your maleness. . . . . "

. . . .

. . . .

"Joe?"

"Yeah, Danny."

"She says she's having sex with me because I'm wonderful and because it's fun."

"Well, Danny, I guess if it's happened before with somebody else, if you have a history of being fucked for kicks, then you're on solid ground. You or the money. It has to be your call."

"Well Joe, we already did it once with me holding a gun on her and she knocked a front tooth of mine out. I guess we could always keep doing it that way and I could keep my eyes open. But you know, and it might sound a little egotistical, but I think I'm going to go with her version of why we're doing so good instead of yours, because otherwise she'd cover up her breasts and I sure don't want her to do that."

"So what else do you have to say?"

"You tired of exchanging love secrets?"

"Correct."

"You want to get Carolyn on the extension. . . . ."

"I'm here. . . . ."

"Is Tish on your end? . . . . ."

"Yeah Joe, I'm here. I just picked up."

"Go ahead then, Danny."

"All right, Joe. You have the money?"

"Yes."

"Why don't you put it in a suitcase or a gym bag, something plain, the smallest thing you can find. And then take out the cost of the bag because we're not giving it back. Now. What time you have?"

". . . . . Not quite a quarter after noon . . . . . thirteen after."

"Okay. Good. Fine. So then at straight-up six this evening, take the money and go to the corner of Ninth and Emerson. It's kind of a nothing little intersection about a block from the main downtown fire station, the big new one on Carter. There's a pay phone on the northeast corner of the intersection. It's inside a plastic shell type of covering near the stoplight. Plenty of meter parking on the street. Shouldn't be too many people still around at six. Just go there and wait. *Both* of you, you understand that? I want both of you by the pay phone at straight-up six this evening, both of you where I can see you. And nobody else."

"This is all. You understand that, don't you, Danny—you're not going to keep coming at us for money, because this is all there is."

"Oh sure, we're professionals here, there's no question about that. And *you* understand that any attempt to pass us harm will be severely dealt with. You're not fucking with part-timers. So just save yourself the disappointment and depression of getting all excited about shooting us and then finding out I'm much too smart for that and would never allow it to happen."

"See you at six, Danny."

"Maybe you will. Maybe not. You just be there."

The pay phone at Ninth and Emerson looked to be a good place for some killing, good as in uncrowded and unsupervised by any variety of cop or guard.

The corner was on the outskirts of a downtown area full of streets that had been turned into malls; malls, they couldn't have killed off downtowns more thoroughly if they'd have closed all the police stations for two weeks. There was no testing done before so many cities had their major arteries blocked, had their streets closed and bricked or tiled in the hope that a green space (bushes, for meditating), and a brown space (benches, for relaxing), and a coping space (a waterfall, for a diversion), would contribute to a carefree open-air shopping and playing atmosphere where the whole family could buy and stroll and eat.

Unfortunately nobody built any partial downtown malls to see what it would be like.

City officials simply saw downtowns losing people and for some reason thought that inconvenience and danger would bring them back. But about the only people downtown malls attracted were those involved in the various monkey businesses, such as practicing sex in public places.

Downtown malls were dangerous because there was no way to adequately police all the dark spots, the alleys and entrances and exits to abandoned or closed businesses.

They were inconvenient because usually you couldn't park anywhere close to where you wanted to go.

And they were illogical because nobody wanted to hang out near where they worked.

So by 6:00 P.M. on average workdays, most downtowns with malls looked like real nice petting zoos with squirrels and birds enjoying the green space set aside by the urban designers, none of whose nicely dressed butts you'd find anywhere near here after dark.

The pay phone on the corner of Ninth and Emerson was a block from a street that had been turned into a mall, and so hardly anybody was around an hour after most work let out. Everybody had bolted for the convenience and security of the suburbs and nobody was nearby except for some members of a religious convention who had come to town to pray, with one of the subjects for tonight's prayer session obviously being a silent call to Jesus for a new chairman for the site selection committee.

Last year they had prayed in Lake Tahoe, which had somehow seemed much more godly.

Joe and Carolyn had the corner pretty much to themselves upon their arrival at eleven minutes of six, finally once and for all resigned to their only course of survival. Nobody's trigger finger shook. Nobody's shooting hand wavered. Nobody's aiming eye twitched. Yet anyhow.

They were going to shoot the bastards coming to take all their money and ruin their lives. This was a war, a life-and-death confrontation. They had done everything possible to keep this unpleasant and potentially untidy scenario from happening. They had tried to reason with the other two. They had even said please. And now they had to defend themselves; it was just that simple.

Making matters tolerable and justifiable was the evil nature of the other two people. They were killers. They did not kill out of rage or panic or self-defense; they killed for money, for greed, and they didn't come any more sinister.

So Joe and Carolyn were willing to accept and deal with the moral ramifications of what was to come. With the right rock and roll on the radio, it felt like it was their civic duty to rid the world of those other two; in fact, standing on the corner at five minutes of six, Joe said he almost felt patriotic.

Joe wore jeans, a long-sleeved weathered T-shirt, and a windbreaker along with some oiled hiking boots from J. Crew. Pre-beat-up shirts cost more than new shirts; Lord, what exactly was the world coming to, besides being great at advertising. Stone-washed? Oh sure. Virgins scrubbing things in a clean-running river.

Carolyn wore jeans and a baggy cotton sweater.

Joe remarked that life was funny because anybody seeing them might have thought they were on their way to watch a wholesome high school or college football game.

Instead he was waiting to shoot somebody right in the middle of his punk face.

Carolyn gave him five; shoot true, baby.

The urge to survive had given them a sense of old school team spirit.

Joe wished aloud that he had taken some target practice. He han't shot a weapon since a duck hunt nine years ago when he was zero hits for eleven shots, with a mallard being the approximate size of a human head.

Carolyn wished aloud that he wouldn't wish aloud: Just don't blink, man, squeeze the rounds off, don't jerk.

Their plan was open-ended and contained the basic premise of shooting the sons of bitches at the first available opportunity.

They had put the money in an athletic workout bag, deducting two hundred dollars for the cost of a thirty-dollar tote, fuck them, anyway.

At three minutes of six, Joe opened the bag and showed Carolyn all the hundred-dollar bills and had her put her arm in there and feel all the money they had, the second-mortgage money, and then he did the same thing. Just *think* of losing this, he said, just think of somebody ripping away what was ours.

Yeah, well, Carolyn thought, I'll think about that right after I get through thinking of you shooting at them and missing and them shooting back and putting you down, with me getting the large insurance payment, as originally planned. As long as Joe started shooting, Carolyn thought with some hopeful anticipation, she should come out of this all right.

So as a part of their new relationship where no feelings about the other would be hidden, she told him what she had been thinking, that for a second she was not torn apart by the possibility of his being riddled in return.

And standing there by the pay phone, he said he understood her feeling, that he was the reason her life and liberty were at stake, and that he bode her no ill will and felt no less encouraged about their future together.

Well that's pretty cool, actually, Carolyn thought, being able to speak her mind without fear or arguing or bitching or preaching; not bad.

And they gave each other five again and felt some true and real hope—maybe they *couldn't* do better than each other, and maybe they *could* improve markedly.

As they were looking ahead with hope and joy, the stupid damn telephone rang.

Joe looked at his watch and saw that his second hand was one second short of exactly six, pretty eerie.

Before answering, once again he said that what he was going to do was shoot the other bastards when they came for the money. If they sent somebody to pick it up, they'd react accordingly and probably force this person to say where the money was going. One way or other this evening, the matter would be resolved as a result of a classic confrontation matching good and evil, exactly the kind of thing that had energized this country and its brave inhabitants since day one.

He wanted a healthy life with Carolyn that was free of obsessions and chock full of vitamins and vegetables, and he was going to have it.

She said that was pretty sweet.

Since this mess had commenced, Joe had felt as though he had just awakened to a world without form, like just after a beloved person had died, a regular in your life; when you woke up, you had to catch up with reality.

But for the first time, and because he was committed to the form of action they had agreed upon, it felt like he belonged here at the pay-phone booth.

Joe kissed Carolyn on the cheek and went to answer the phone.

She stopped him and returned the favor, put it back on his lips.

JOE AND DANNY ON THE TELEPHONE
Joe on this pay phone; Danny on a pay phone atop a nearby hill. With binoculars, 6:01 P.M.

"Hello."

"Joe?"

"Yeah."

"Danny here. You're doing fine so far. Is that the money your wife has there with her in the bag?"

"Yeah."

"All right. Now what I want both of you to do is get in the car and drive to Fifth and Carson. It's not far at all, about two miles, two and a quarter, tops. Make a left on Carson and go a block and a half. That would be north. What's there is the police station, the main downtown branch or whatever you want to call it. I want—"

"The *police station*—"

"Just listen. You can ask questions in a minute. I want you to go in the main entrance to the police station, which is off Carson. Double glass doors. They're about right in the middle of the block, between Fifth and Sixth. Just go inside and keep going straight to a central lobby area. You'll go in the main glass doors off Carson, you'll go straight down a hallway, oh, fifty yards, and there'll be a place where the other entrances to the building come together in that central lobby area. It's like an intersection, four hallways meeting. The way you come in, there's a sign when you get to the lobby that says Homicide with an arrow pointing to the left. Right is the Arson Division. Now beneath the Homicide sign there's a beat-up wooden bench, it's like from an old police station or something. Six or seven feet long. Pretty banged around. Armrests on each end. It's exactly beneath the Homicide sign. What I want you two to do is go right this second and get in your car there and drive straight to the downtown police station and sit on the old wooden bench beneath the Homicide sign. Put the money right on your lap. The bag. And sit there and wait. There's plenty of parking on the street all around the police station. Should be open spots all over the place this time of the evening. If there aren't any parking places on the street, there's a pay lot right across the way, directly in front, all right? You got it? . . . . . "

" . . . . Hello? . . . . "

"Joe?"

" . . . . Hello? I can't hear you, it must be a bad connection, something must be wrong with this old pay phone. . . . . "

"Joe, don't try any bullshit junk like that, looking to buy some time to think of a way around this because I've stunned you so much. Listen, there is only one way that this can go and that's my way. You made the effort. Hell of a try. So now it's done. I tried that phone. This phone. Both phones. So I know they all work. So now get your butts in that car and get to the police station and sit on the goddamn wooden bench under the Homicide sign."

" . . . . . All right."

"Now listen, if it turns out you do have to pull into the pay lot across the street, just go ahead and take a couple of bucks right off the top of our money there to cover it. I think it's a buck seventy-five an hour, right around there. You don't need to leave a receipt. We trust you perfect."

*   *   *

Joe and Carolyn had several things to decide before entering the downtown police station located on Carson between Fifth and Sixth Streets.

The first was whether or not they should carry an unregistered and illegal firearm into the police station.

God Almighty, Lord, what if they had a metal detector or something like that in there. Weren't there some courtrooms upstairs that had to be protected? Losing their money would be bad enough. Broke *and* arrested—oh stop, nobody deserved that.

But Carolyn's point was that it would be very hard to shoot somebody without a gun.

Joe said nobody was shooting anybody inside a police station, a fact that depressed the both of them, so he left the pistol in the car that had been parked out front at a meter at the curb.

Taking money from somebody dangerous inside a police station, not a bad way to get rich, Carolyn said as she slouched onto the old and splintered bench beneath the Homicide sign, as instructed.

Joe shrugged and said maybe, it was still early. It looked good but maybe not *that* good.

Carolyn wanted to know why not that good, and so Joe set about thinking why exchanging money in a police station so you wouldn't be hurt or killed wasn't great, but he couldn't think of a reason and became even more depressed than when he had to leave the damn pistol outside.

After they had sat on the bench beneath the Homicide sign for about two downbeat minutes, a uniformed officer from an information desk across the way walked over and asked if he could be of assistance.

Joe, whose face had been buried in his hands as he sat trying to think of some harm he could do to somebody coming for their money in a police station, looked up and said no, they were fine, they were just waiting for an acquaintance.

The cop nodded and went back to his information desk.

Several minutes after that Danny and Tish showed up look-

ing like somebody off *The Dating Game,* arm in arm, his right
around her shoulders, her left arm around his waist.

Tish wore a short skirt.

Danny's mood was as up as Joe's was not.

He said hey what's going on and held out his hand to shake
Joe's but nothing came from the other side.

Joe instead looked away.

Carolyn sighed.

Danny got down on his haunches like a baseball catcher and
spoke softly and said there was no need to get so pissed off and
hold grudges just because they had been left *not* holding the
bag.

Then he laughed.

And Tish reached out and thumped the top of his head with
the middle finger of her right hand and said you stop that right
now, you quit teasing them.

Danny looked up at her and nodded.

Turned back to Joe and Carolyn.

Said that at least now as they began to reconstruct their relationship, they could concentrate on the things that really mat-
tered like trust and openness because they sure as hell wouldn't
have any excess money to worry about.

Tish couldn't help but laugh a little at that one.

Next, Danny unzipped the gym bag and looked inside at all
the hundreds and showed Tish, who got to her toes and kissed
her man on the corner of his mouth, using the tip of her tongue,
a pretty common thing to do in public.

Danny and Tish both had new wigs on and looked much different than before.

His wig was straight, hers curly.

Joe and Carolyn sank deeper into the hard wooden bench,
not an easy thing to do.

Danny said here was what would happen now. *Nothing,* as
far as Joe and Carolyn were concerned. They would sit right
there on the bench for ten minutes. Then they could do what-

ever they wished, go relate, stop and smell the truth, they could do all the things people in relationships based on brains did. The tapes of each person hiring the murder of the other would be returned on the morrow, then everybody could get back to hanging in there some more.

Tish leaned over and said that if either of them ever needed anybody else left alive, *please* be sure and drop them a line.

She laughed.

Then she and Danny walked out the front door with the bag with all the money in it.

They stopped and waved at the front door, and seemed to be giggling as they did.

Joe started to give them the finger but decided not to give them any *more* pleasure, so he waved so long in return.

They began their ten-minute wait as instructed and made some plans for the immediate future as best they were able.

Carolyn told Joe to sell the motherfucking gun; they shouldn't lose more than fifty on that exchange.

She'd become a high-class whore, charging five hundred to a thousand per hour, screwing many of her former friends and co-workers. He could dynamite open some remote cash tellers, just blow off the fronts and reach in and take out what money there was.

Joe's thoughts about their futures were considerably more re-strained. Carolyn asked what they were. Joe said that the first thing in the morning, they could start with some relationship counseling.

They could sit down and formulate a budget, see what they had to cut back on and by how much; get the house ready for selling.

Then after that, they could start participating in some new interests, bicycling, possibly, join a book club.

Then tomorrow night, maybe a game of bingo somewhere, get lucky, pick up a few dollars.

As Carolyn put her hands over her face and started weeping

softly and admitted that she was once again having thoughts about paying somebody to shoot him for the insurance money, a cop walked up and asked Joe if that had been Charley Mook with the salty-looking woman in the uplifting skirt.

JOE AND CAROLYN WITH THE COP IN THE POLICE
STATION COFFEE SHOP
Joe and Carolyn on one side of the booth, the cop on the
other; Joe speaks with him, 6:35 P.M.

"Out there in the lobby, you asked if that had been Charley
somebody. Charley who?"
　　"Mook. M double-o k, pronounced like the cow sound."
　　"Wasn't who Charley Mook? Which person did you mean?"
　　"The fellow you were talking to. Black knit shirt. With the
woman wearing what appeared to be a shirttail for a skirt."
　　"Well, actually, I don't know him really well. He's just a
passing acquaintance. He said his name was Danny."
　　"Could have been."
　　"Who's Charley Mook?"
　　"He used to run a club on Central. Not exactly a meeting
place for the clergy. Now the hair on the guy you were talking
to . . . . . "
　　"It was a wig."
　　"Yeah? Well, you know, I only saw him from halfway across
the lobby, but the size was right, and the cheekbones. But
mostly it was the way he carried himself. Kind of a smart-ass
attitude, if you know what I mean."
　　"Excuse me."
　　"This is my wife, Carolyn."
　　"Hello."

"Hi. Listen, Who owned the place on Central? The restaurant. Club."

"I think it was an uncle. A throwback to the days of handmade craftsmanship. You know what I mean. Choking. Like that. He's in prison, last I heard—couple of years on tax evasion."

"It's him, Joe."

"Good Christ, good heavens . . . . ."

"One more thing, Officer."

"What's that, Carolyn?"

"Do you think you could find an address for this Charley Mook?"

"Probably. What do you need it for?"

"Oh. We just want to drop off a surprise engagement gift. Nothing urgent."

Charley Mook was Danny, all right, because the new white Range Rover was beside the house in the driveway, a pretty tempting place to leave a vehicle that valuable.

Joe thought about stealing a hubcap or two on the way inside, set Danny back half a thousand, *had* to be worth at the very least a couple hundred a cap.

The house next to the Range Rover was a pretty nice one, stylish without being pretentious. The whole neighborhood appeared to be expensive enough, with homes all around ranging in price, Joe guessed, from one-fifty to three hundred thousand. Signs posted at the corners said the neighbors watched carefully for people who didn't belong there, nervous people like Joe and Carolyn; so once on that block, Joe put his arm around her and smiled and tried to look harmless.

The house they wanted in was a white brick one that was longer from front to back than it was side to side. It was surrounded by some large trees, pecans, many of which had fallen and were underfoot. The house had no particular style; American was as good a description as any.

It was dark when they got there.

After spotting the white Range Rover, they went by the house in one direction and then turned around at the first intersection and came back the other way, noticing but one light on inside, or a couple of faint ones, coming from the middle of the home.

Joe parked his car three blocks away by a small park and they walked back toward Danny's, guessing at what might be the fastest and safest way into the place.

The gun was inside Joe's right front windbreaker pocket.

The windows and doors at Danny's house had stickers on them saying that an electronic security system was in place and was active.

Going in through a door or a window was dangerous beyond the possibility of an alarm because they had no idea what was on the other side.

So they eliminated the possibility of smashing something with the gun.

This seemed to be the safest and most reasonable of their choices: Carolyn would stand up straight on the front porch, acting like she belonged there, and would just go ahead and knock right on the door and, once admitted, would say that she had gotten the address from the cop who had recognized Danny, exactly the way it had happened. And then she would ask for some extortion money in order not to tell Joe that she had found them.

After she was inside and talking about serious matters like money, Joe would join her, pistol at the ready.

Perhaps even a simpler way would be to have Carolyn talk her way inside and, instead of waiting for Joe to muscle in and join her, she could take the pistol from a hidden place and shoot both of them right on the spot.

But Joe was worried that it would be asking too much of Carolyn, even though she said she could handle it fine and trusted herself more than she did him, and was probably a better shot, and was probably mentally tougher, also.

So they quickly thought it over, walking from their car to Danny's.

Would she need him in there?

Was there something essential that he could provide?

No.

Therefore it was agreed upon that Carolyn would do it alone, would at least start it alone, with Joe supporting her quickly from the rear—she was going to act like a blackmailer to the blackmailers. *Jesus,* did a hot bubble bath sound good. But before it could happen, Carolyn had to shoot Danny and then his fancy-legged girlfriend.

Anxious to get back to their own lives, and with their own money, and eager to be forgiven for what had to be done, they each went up the front steps quietly, on their toes; and Joe quickly stepped off the porch among some tall yews and firs.

Before knocking, Carolyn tried the doorknob almost as an afterthought, like a kid looking into a pay phone coin slot for change, wishing for luck but not expecting it.

And the front door had been left unlocked, just the kind of thing a couple of people in a good mood would do, just run in to celebrate a success with no mind for the routine of security; plus, Danny of course thought he was a snake.

Finding the front door unlocked, Carolyn motioned for Joe to get out of the yews and come see for himself.

And so he did.

Carolyn took a deep breath and opened the front door half an inch, wished for no squeaks, then pushed it in another inch or so.

With Joe's head over hers, they each put an eye to the crack and squinted inside the house where all their money was.

The only light that was on was not nearby, yet its glow partially illuminated the area just inside the front door, showing a hallway running straight back into the dwelling, with doors and doorways opening left and right off of it.

There was a fork at the end of the main hallway, left probably being the central living area, as that doorway opening appeared larger, wider, and taller than the others; to the right was the light.

There was no television noise, no radio sounds, no clocks ticking, just something like a soft whir from a refrigerator coming from due left.

There was, though, a dog just inside the front door, a tiny thing that looked like a ball of lint, a Pomeranian, Carolyn whispered to Joe; her aunt had one.

The Pomeranian was facing away from the door no more than a yard away, sleeping, it seemed.

With the dog there, they couldn't get the door open enough to slide inside.

Carolyn whispered to Joe that what he should do was very slowly reach inside and grab the dog, grab it by the mouth and hold it closed, and yank the animal outside, then she'd run it to the corner and toss it in somebody else's yard for a while.

And that was what Joe aimed to do, slowly extending his hand, an inch at a time until it was over and slightly behind the Pomeranian's little head.

Sensing Joe's presence, or seeing a shadow from a little moonlight coming in a front window, or smelling his hand, the Pomeranian looked up suddenly and in one fast motion dug its needlelike teeth into the fleshy part of Joe's right hand between the thumb and first finger.

Which hurt.

Blood spurted.

Joe opened his mouth but didn't scream and grabbed the Pomeranian and jerked it out the door and ran from the porch, down the sidewalk, and into the street, where he threw the dog as hard as he could up into a dense old magnolia tree that was in the front yard across the way.

The tiny dog caught in the tree, stayed up there, and growled a little bit.

Joe returned to the porch and told Carolyn what had happened. She smiled and kissed the place where he had been bitten. She told him it was still quiet in there. Joe nodded. Caught his breath. Rubbed some more blood off on his shirt. He whispered to her that what they'd do now was creep into the house and proceed down the hallway toward the source of the light coming from the rear of the dwelling. Carolyn whispered fine, now don't forget to take your damn gun out. Joe said he was slightly worried about shooting somebody innocent in these unknown surroundings and jittery circumstances. Carolyn said that she doubted anybody too innocent would be hanging with *these* two; but if he had to shoot without knowing where he was shooting, or precisely whom, aim low with the first one.

So Joe tiptoed down the hallway with Carolyn right behind him. The floors in the house were wood and squeaked once halfway to the end of the hall, causing both of them to stop walking and breathing.

After a few seconds, Carolyn whispered that if they walked close to the wall, the wood slats on the floor would be less flexible there and less likely to make any noise.

And she was right, they were able to move the length of the hall and reach the door of the master bedroom without making another sound.

Across the way, a large mutt had heard the noise in the magnolia tree and had gone there thinking a cat might be handy and was surprised to find the Pomeranian instead.

The mutt said a dog in a tree was about the limpest thing he had ever seen.

The Pomeranian said he hadn't been chased there, he had been fucking thrown there, now help him down.

The mutt said forget it and went to get some friends to come see the Pomeranian up the magnolia.

They communicated with their eyes and with body language.

Tish was in bed reading a magazine.

Alone.

The cash had been emptied out of the gym bag and was on the bed and floor. It appeared that they had been rolling in the hundred-dollar bills—and probably laughing.

On the far side of the bedroom, shower sounds came from a bathroom, and also some steam.

Guessing that those two had been having sex on their money, Joe stepped immediately and angrily into the bedroom, the gun held at arm's length and pointed at Tish, and he told her not to move.

She was very surprised to see somebody she had just screwed out of a lot of money jump into her bedroom wanting it back. She pulled up the sheet and covered her bare breasts, which had appeared naturally lovely and free flowing and not weighted through surgery performed on any insecurities.

Joe frowned at the pulled-up sheet.

Tish tossed aside the magazine she had been reading and asked Joe what was going on. He said oh, not much, they were going door to door through the entire city looking to get their money back, guessing that it would take at least four years and probably something closer to six and a half; and you talk about luck, they had come upon this house on the *second block* after they started.

Carolyn joined Joe by the bed and asked where Danny was and Tish nodded toward the bathroom.

Joe nodded and went and got him.

It was pretty simple.

Danny was in the shower, washing his hair.

The shower door opened outward. Joe swung it wide, and Danny, hearing the latch, grinned and held out his hand, obviously thinking it was his woman there. And Joe thought about putting something very unexpected in Danny's hand. But he decided not to waste any effort or brains on getting cute and said instead here's a towel unless you choose to die naked.

Danny quit grinning, ran some water on his face, washed away the shampoo, then squinted at Joe.

The first thing he asked was if Tish was all right, actually a pretty sweet thing for a person in real trouble to do.

Joe said Tish was fine and smiled.

Danny asked what he meant by that. Was that a sexual reference? Her breasts were fine? What was fine?

Joe said it took some courage being jealous into a gun and told him Tish was fine any way you looked at her, emotionally or physically.

By the time Danny got some clothes on and he and Joe got back into the bedroom, Carolyn had most of the money picked up and counted and stacked.

Danny sat on the bed beside Tish and took her hand and told her not to worry and to please keep the sheet up.

Joe said the sheet didn't matter because he was going to shoot them where they sat. He explained that he and Carolyn weren't going to live in trepidation, waiting for more extortion demands, more threats. They were going to do the world a big favor by reducing by two the number of its health hazards.

Joe raised the pistol and pointed it at Danny's mouth as Carolyn nodded and said yeah, go on, *do* it.

Danny yelled *wait*. Joe said what, what. Danny yelled that he had something important to say. Which was pretty obvious. Last words were always considered important.

So Joe lowered the gun a little out of courtesy.

Told Danny to go on, say it, say whatever.

Danny said you can't kill us.

Joe cleared his throat. Asked if that was it.

Danny . . . nodded. Shrugged.

Joe looked at Tish and said she was next as he raised the gun once more and pointed it at Danny.

Tish said you can't kill us because God would not like it and you would spend eternity in a raging hell.

Joe kept the gun right on Danny's mouth and said he certainly could kill killers if they had no recourse. They had researched it in church and had but to ask forgiveness and give themselves to the Lord afterward, both of which they looked forward to doing.

Danny yelled *hang on* and told them that there had been a mistake with that, *he* had never killed anybody in his life.

Tish quickly nodded and said she wasn't really a bad person, either; this was her first attempt at killing for money. She had been a receptionist at an advertising agency before.

Danny told them that he had helped run a restaurant that went broke.

Joe didn't believe that they hadn't killed anybody and told Carolyn that they were only playing good to save their lives. He took a step closer to Danny and cocked the trigger on the pistol.

But Carolyn quickly moved between Joe and Danny and said just a second, she couldn't have a hand in killing regular people just trying something different. They had to check it out first, for God's sake, see if they were what they said, see if they were in actuality nobodies.

What was five minutes, anyway; get something to eat out of the icebox.

So Joe called his bookmaker Cooper and asked him about this woman from Kansas City, Tish. He said he'd like to know something about her background. If she had a history in killing, if she was any good at it, for example. Cooper, who had the eighteen thousand coming, plus what Joe's gun had cost, four hundred, wanted to know what was wrong. He sounded put-out, anxious, eager to be paid what was getting longer overdue by the minute. Joe said oh, please don't misunderstand him. Nothing was wrong. They were getting on fine, he and Tish. She was very attentive. Sincere. The business that would enable Cooper to get his money was proceeding as scheduled. He told his bookmaker that he was developing a slight crush on the woman and wanted to know what she was made of, that was all, he didn't want to get too carried away with the devil. Cooper said in that case, all right, he'd tell Joe a few things. Tish was his cousin who had gotten tired of marrying rich men and was going after divorce-sized dollars in another way, in this way. When pressed about the subject of experience, Cooper said yeah, this was her first job of such a nature. And he wanted to know how she was doing.

Couldn't be better, Joe said.

Next, Danny gave Joe and Carolyn his ex-girlfriend's, Dee Dee's, telephone number, and they called her and learned that Danny had beaten up quite a few people while he was managing the restaurant, but to the best of her recollection, he had never buried anybody.

Dee Dee told them to tell Danny that she had found somebody new and that they were very happy and that her new boyfriend knew kick-boxing in case he was thinking about sniffing around.

God Almighty, you talk about not being able to get good help, Joe thought, hanging up.

After learning that the two people sitting close together in bed had never killed a single soul in their whole surprising lives, Carolyn went to the kitchen and got something to drink from the refrigerator and then she and her husband took a break on a sofa in a sitting area off the master bedroom.

Joe put his arm around his wife's shoulder and they sat tilting down some beer and looking at Danny and Tish and wondering what they were supposed to do now.

They didn't want those two on the bed to come after their money anymore.

But those two probably would.

Wouldn't they?

But they couldn't shoot beginners.

Could they?

JOE AND DANNY
At Bloomers on Conchita Street, Santa Fe, in a small
unfinished office, with the walls needing paint and other
decorating

"Danny?"

"My good friend. Speak."

"Got a second?"

"Yeah, sure, Joe. I'm just watering these yellow things."

"Peonies."

"Those are the ones."

"Danny, listen, I want to try an idea out on you before the grand opening starts."

"No problem."

"I was thinking that we could try to specialize whenever possible, you know, with the customers. Concentrate on a specific type of person. Develop a pitch for a customer and stay with it, perfect it."

"Sounds good to me. I'll take the nineteen-year-old pot-smoking sluts. . . . ."

"Now listen to me. What you need to do is take the older women. You've got a great natural charm with them."

"Yeah?"

"Sure. You're a good listener. And you're full of it and dislike a lot, which is what older people do for a hobby. We'll come up with a list of what they're pissed off about. Tourists. Government. Flowers are like grandkids to old women, and God knows who winds up with all the money."

"Fine with me, Joe. I'll have them up to their butts in begonias."

CAROLYN AND TISH
By the front door at the flower shop

"Carolyn?"

"Yeah."

"Come here. Look out front. Black Porsche."

"So?"

"That's the one I was telling you about. Clark."

"Oh Jesus."

"Why don't you take him today."

"Oh God, no, please. I'll bag the garbage every day for a month."

"Come on. Roll up your cut-off jeans one more time. He's been talking to me about our landscaping his whole *ranch.*"

"But he looks like a forty-five-year-old frat rat. . . . ."

"Carolyn, now listen to me. These sons and daughters of rich parents are going to be the lifeblood of our business. I had lunch with that shrink around the corner, Liz what's-her-name, yesterday, and we went all over this. People like Clark have no talent or skills and are insecure about their wealth beyond comprehension. They know that if it weren't for their family businesses, they couldn't get jobs raking. The grand old pioneers of this country are dying off and their inheritors and their incompetence offer us a unique investment opportunity. About all they have that's real are their fantasies. Pretty funny, huh.

So we have to praise their smarts and instead of one fantasy, me, let's give this guy two."

"But how could anybody be interested in anything these bores have to say, Tish?"

"Think of their interests as being business opportunities. This one, the one from the Porsche, is a fly fisherman. All you do with any of that bullshit is act like what he is doing is hard. A little touch on the forearm. A smile. After we've sold them a semi-full of flowers marked up three hundred percent, the hell with them."

"Well. I'd sure rather bag refuse."

So now with their flower shop that they made out of an abandoned gas station in a nowhere part of town going great, now that they were partners right down the center, there was no need for killing.

No need for extorting.

Their only need was a bigger cash register; after an impatiens sale, they had to put overflow money in a flowerpot.

The comingling worked well, with each person contributing a unique strength to the partnership.

Danny was a strong physical presence, good for security and selling to senior women, and he was amazing at getting great deals on flowers, large quantities of them.

Their last load of vinca, a thorough and attractive groundcover, had arrived on a truck with no license plate at a quarter of three in the morning and was unloaded by men with no English. Anybody trying to chase down something that quickly changed appearance naturally, something that grew fast, well, it would be like trying to track a cheeseburger.

Danny was a big gambler and did it in front of Joe; and whereas Joe thought it would be good therapy, sitting back and watching the perils of inevitable doom grind a person down, Danny got on a hot streak and won eleven thousand dollars.

Carolyn was in charge of all things practical and ran the

books. The old gas station cost next to nothing to rent, and it was Carolyn's idea to get it and go by the *Field of Dreams* philosophy where location was secondary to charm.

Tish was better with people than anybody Joe and Carolyn had ever seen, an old-time throwback to creative sales experts who could read a customer in a second and customize an appropriate approach.

She was good with men, very good, selling them astounding amounts of flowers, a fact that sometimes pissed off Danny. There had almost been a little violence several times, the fly fisherman from the Porsche, for example: Danny had once told him to keep his hands off Tish's arms or he'd cut off one of his fingers and put it in one of those slots meant for cigars on those cocksucker-type fly-fishing shirts with twenty-eight pockets and nine zippers.

Tish did not deal with Danny as suggested by any of the 5,409 self-help books currently on the market. She didn't try to develop trust, any of that cheap pulp fiction. Say she wanted his jealousy to cease. The way she saw it, there were two ways to get a satisfactory result: education or threats. To educate him would take many years of hard work and she didn't have the time. So she told him to keep the jealousy to himself or she would throw his ass right out the door and go attend to the other guy's fly. If he shut up, and stayed shut up, maybe it would dawn on him that there was no reason to waste time on nonessential emotions.

Danny hadn't been jealous in more than five weeks, far and away a personal best.

Joe was in charge of the creative end of the business. And he was good at it, naming the flower shop Bloomers. But sometimes he got fancy with their ads in the newspaper and showed off with big words, which was counterproductive and cost more.

And, Lord above, was Santa Fe ever touristy and growing more so by the hour, and as such, was the perfect spot to hustle flowers. Not that there could be a bad place. Nothing held the universal appeal of flowers. Affordable to the poor, a colorful pot could cheer a dump.

And of course the rich folks had to have their flowers to keep up.

Santa Fe was being overwhelmed by Californians bailing out before something ate them. And though overimpressed by their own knowledge, whatever it was, Californians spent the money on flowers. What they had taken for granted before bailing, birds-of-paradise growing up through cracks on Santa Monica Boulevard, they now had to re-create.

There was not a lot of producing land to live off of in and around Santa Fe unless you were an anteater.

It was similar to other pretty places on sorry-ass soil in that its scenery was paramount and in that its population was comprised primarily of retired people who couldn't see far enough to know it was so touristy.

Santa Fe was industrial-strength artsy-fartsy unless you were a merchant, in which case its cultural ambience became relevant, pertinent, wonderful, and reasonably priced.

Hack artists were drawn to Santa Fe like gamblers to a crap shoot.

A few good artists lived there and gave the minutely talented more hope than they deserved.

On an average business day in Santa Fe, a buying frenzy existed.

Joe and Carolyn were hard at it on a daily basis, trying to make their relationship work; sometimes to Joe it seemed like an uphill battle, barefoot. But they would see.

Joe and Carolyn's new life together was going something like this: They were eating well and exercising and taking up new interests like yoga.

Joe had a new bisexual friend, a woman artist named Mary, who painted desert animals like lizards and vultures with oversized sex organs on them. Pretty weird. Hanging with bisexual artists who couldn't draw hands very well—which was the sign of a good artist, drawing good hands was—wasn't Joe's favorite pastime. But he hoped the new interest would be symbolic of his desire to keep moving.

He went to Gamblers Anonymous, Carolyn to Alcoholics Anonymous. She loved going to recovery groups, but Joe didn't particularly, finding them slightly cultish with their elements of brainwashing wherein everybody said the same things together, leaving little room for individual creativity.

The Santa Fe chapter of Gamblers Anonymous was held in a gazebo in a tree arboretum in a city park and consisted of six people besides Joe, all men close to their seventies. Basically what they did was sit around and goddamn the devilishly bad luck that had plagued their gambling days and had driven them to this depressing place.

It was his misfortune to have as a compulsion something that wasn't cool to recover from.

Joe and Carolyn also went to relationship counseling once a week.

They had been through three counselors and were starting on their fourth. What Joe didn't like about counseling so far was most counselors were former addicts; they counseled from experience at being sick. And whereas counseling about healing was good, Joe wanted somebody to tell him what being *normal* felt like. He was aware of nutty. All he wanted was a counselor who had experience with sanity.

So they were plowing along, Carolyn armed with an endless quiver of boundaries to protect her various needs. Joe could have sworn that he heard somewhere that boundaries were supposed to be used in good faith and in good as well as sorry times. But it seemed like many times Carolyn brought her boundaries out like crime scene tape.

But oh well, hell with it, Joe decided, to each his or her whatever.

Sometimes it seemed like working on their relationship took more time than living their relationship did.

Danny and Tish continued to base their relationship around play, primarily sex. Neither showed any sign of tiring of sex, either. Danny had never become bored with masturbation, so how could he get bored experiencing the same feeling with a beautiful and nasty woman?

No way, he had to believe.

They had their serious time, too. Important relationship issues like Danny's predisposal, and current disposal, to try to control certain aspects of Tish's life, like which movies she should prefer, were discussed in detail. They reserved a special time for discussing meaningful relationship matters—during sex. The night before last, for example, as they stood fucking on their deck overlooking a mesa turning pink with the sunset, Tish said listen friend, quit telling me what I should think about actors and acting. *Get* it? Danny said oh Jesus yes, oh God yes, he got it, he had it, *please* forgive me, I'll never do it again; and so far after these intimate conversations, his word had been his bond.

All four of them agreed that it would be fascinating to see where free and open and truthful communication would fit best in a relationship, before or after sex.

Joe started making some notes about all their lives.

Dictating into a tape.

Maybe it would be a book someday.

But if any of this was ever printed, wouldn't that mean his relationship had failed, because wasn't the best reading always about getting your butt kicked?